"*The Recollection*, Cherie Dargan's fourth novel set in Jubilee Junction, Iowa, charms readers even as it propels us forward to solve the mystery of a quilt connecting two families and two eras in history. Whether one is a middle-school reader discovering for the first time how people adapted to the Depression or an adult reader remembering stories from their grandparents, *The Recollection* will delight and surprise. While some in Depression-era Jubilee Junction are battered by farm foreclosure and the shame of going to the town school in tattered farm clothes, others crave purpose and connection in life. The present-day sleuths find that these ancestors' needs fit together like the pieces of a quilt. As these teachers and librarians investigate old newspapers, old photos, and old relatives, they learn important lessons for resolving the present-day fissures troubling Jubilee Junction."

~Dr. Julie Husband
Professor, Department of Languages and Literatures
University of Northern Iowa

"Anyone looking for a charming Christmas novella will enjoy *The Recollection*. The backdrop of The Great Depression adds an extra touch of sentimental value and nostalgia to the season. Family mysteries are discovered when someone spots a unique quilt, that they've seen in another place! This dual timeline story addresses the long forgotten era of prohibition, simple country Christmas, and the undying love of family."

~Dr. Ambri Refer, DMIN
Assistant Director, Hudson, Iowa, Public Library

"Once again, Cherie Dargan has stitched history, love, loss and triumph into story form, with a little laughter and a few tears along the way. *The Recollection* of the Crazy Quilt is a beautiful story, a patchwork of family and friends we've come to know and love in this fourth novel set in Jubilee Junctions. Readers will enjoy delving deep into the heartaches and strong-willed spirit of the Great Depression as they follow along with modern-day newlyweds, David and Gracie on the trail to solve yet another family quilt mystery. Happy reading!"

~Sheri Smith Shonk,
Author of the Houses of Hope series

"*The Recollection* is a wonderful patchwork of hard times, redemption, and mysteries. Who we are and how we got here are universal questions, but sometimes parts of our family history are blocked out. Just as in a quilt, many pieces constitute the whole. Chasing the unknowns will have you so engrossed that you will probably make this a "one-sitting read." I wish you joy in the journey."

~Judith Robl, Author of
As Grandma Says

"*The Promise* is a dual-time novel that addresses themes of human trafficking and racial prejudice, as well as healing after depression and suffering loss. Newlywed Gracie is given a cedar chest with a false bottom, holding letters from World War I, a wedding dress, and Grandma Mary's Wedding Ring Quilt. But why would a family member object to having any of it displayed in a WWI exhibit so many decades later? A compelling mystery for Gracie to resolve."

~Joy Neal Kidney, author of
the Leora's Stories series

"Strangers in family photographs and two identical Depression-era Crazy Quilts trigger a new mystery for Gracie—a lost family story of repeated rescue, a story of mending the tears of the Great Depression. Dargan offers hope here for dark times."

~Dr. Barbara Lounsberry, Author of
Virginia Woolf Diaries trilogy

"*Grandmother's Treasures: Book Three, The Promise*, takes readers on a spirited road trip with newlyweds David and Gracie as they trace the path of family history, uncovering never before known details attached to yet another family quilt. If you like dual-timeline reads with twists and turns, interesting glimpses of American history, and poignant family relationships, *The Promise* will leave you satisfied and smiling. Enjoy!"

Sheri Smith Shonk, Author of
the Houses of Hope series

"Dargan connects all the dots, weaving her dual timeline featuring Grace in the present and Mary in the past during WW I. [*The Promise*] brims with rich, well-researched history, and it's easy to follow the changing eras, each with its daunting challenges. Midwesterners, in particular, will love the vibe and feel at home on the pages of *The Promise*.

~Patti Stockdale, Author of
Three Little Things and His Treasured Bride

"I love the history of the honeymoon and its juxtaposition to a modern form of slavery. My grandmother was a quilter, and I've helped her, pieced a baby quilt of my own, and am starting another for my eldest daughter's only daughter who is due in June. My mother was the genealogist in our family, and I've inherited her work, which I've not had time to maintain. This was a fun read for all those reasons."

~Judith Robl, Speaker and Author

"As with Cherie's debut novel, this story [*The Legacy*] intermingles Civil War history and modern-day events, a strong combination."

~Gail Kittleson, author of
The Winds of Change

"Cherie Dargan delivers a second charming historical cozy in *Grandmother's Treasures Book 2: The Legacy*. In this dual timeline book, a bloodstained Civil War Era family quilt stirs a search for answers rooted in mystery and history. War, injustice, danger, romance, and reconciliation—How could a reader ask for more?"

~Shelly Beach, Christy Award winning co-author of
Love Letters from the Edge

"I love this story! Cherie Dargan can sure paint a beautiful word picture! She spins a gorgeous adventure in the first installment of her *Grandmother's Treasures* series where she treats us to an up-close look at one of her personal family stories in *The Gift*. I, for one, am grateful. It's a colorful, lush and adventurous story, infused with grit, determination, and gutsy, likable characters (especially the females!). Her descriptive style had me craving corn muffins and chili as well as traveling and travailing with her on her journey of discovery. I would highly recommend this book and I can't wait for the next in the series!"
~Wanda Sanchez, Christy Award winning co-author of
Love Letters from the Edge

"*The Gift* is a peek into an Iowa farm family. It pieces the present day and past into a quilt filled with details about World War 2. Through the eyes of Gracie, the main character, readers see how past trauma and life choices impact family relationships for generations to come. Those who enjoy books about family, quilting, and the 1940s will find this one to be a comfortable read."
~Jolene Philo, Author of
Does My Child Have PTSD?

"Cherie Dargan captured my imagination with the first heartwarming book in her five-part *Grandmother's Treasures* series, *The Gift*. It was inspired by her marvelous collection of antique quilts and other heirlooms and the strong women in her family, especially her mom and aunts, who have been Dargan's lodestars."
~Melody Parker, Author of
"Five Memorable Stories"—*Waterloo Courier*

the recollection

Book 4
The Recollection
Cherie Dargan
"Share what you have and trust Jesus to multiply the loaves and fishes."
marie 1933

GRANDMOTHER'S TREASURES
BOOK 4

the recollection

a dual time-line Christmas novel

CHERIE DARGAN

WordCrafts Press

The Recollection
Copyright © 2025
Cherie Dargan

Hardback ISBN: 978-1-967649-05-1
Paperback ISBN: 978-1-967649-06-8

Cover concept and design by Mike Parker

Map & Family Tree designed by Patricia Tiffany Morris for Tiffany Inks Studio LLC

Published by WordCrafts Press
Cody, Wyoming 82414
www.wordcrafts.net

For my Grandpa Lee Lewis—farmer, truck driver, and builder—who built a truck house and took his family on an adventure in 1928. It's also dedicated to the memory of Grandma Nellie and Great-Grandma Eva, and to all their grandchildren (My cousins Jim, Ed, Jon, & Richard; my big sister Cathi; and cousins Charlene, Lee, Tom & Anne).

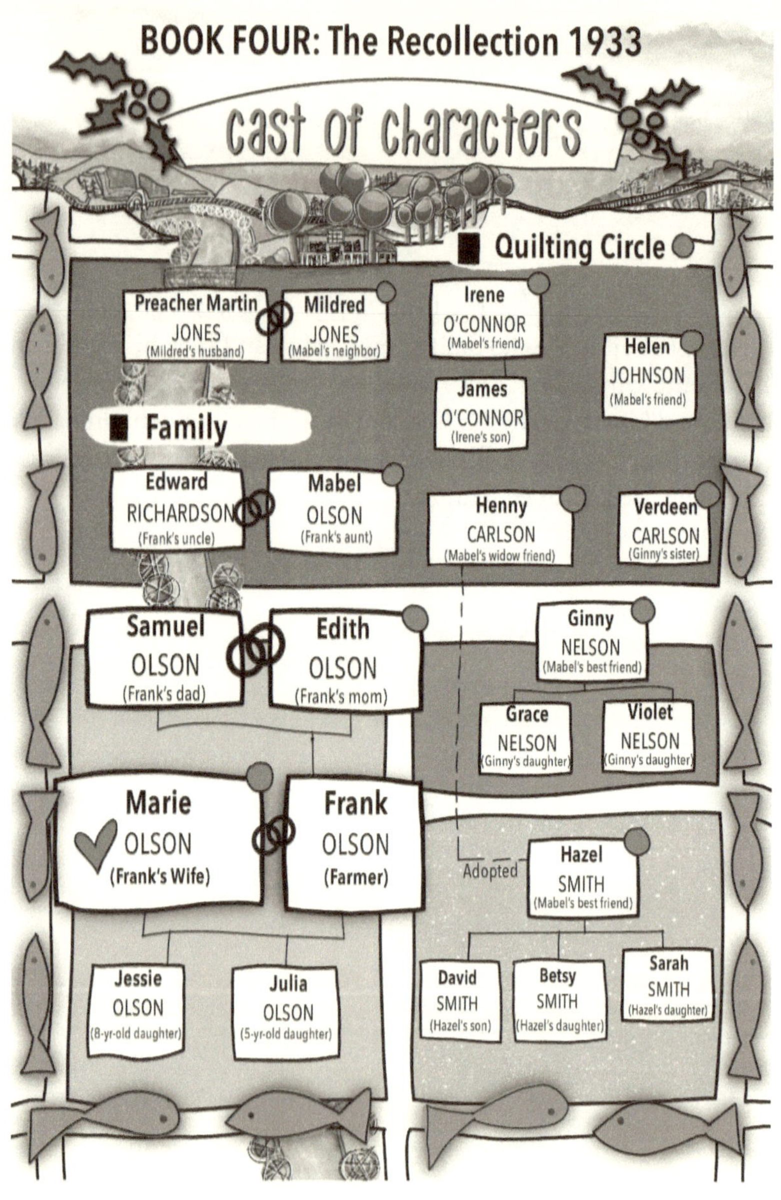

BOOK FOUR: The Recollection 1933
cast of characters
Quilting Circle
Preacher Martin JONES (Mildred's husband)
Mildred JONES (Mabel's neighbor)
Irene O'CONNOR (Mabel's friend)
Helen JOHNSON (Mabel's friend)
James O'CONNOR (Irene's son)
Family
Edward RICHARDSON (Frank's uncle)
Mabel OLSON (Frank's aunt)
Henny CARLSON (Mabel's widow friend)
Verdeen CARLSON (Ginny's sister)
Samuel OLSON (Frank's dad)
Edith OLSON (Frank's mom)
Ginny NELSON (Mabel's best friend)
Grace NELSON (Ginny's daughter)
Violet NELSON (Ginny's daughter)
Marie OLSON (Frank's Wife)
Frank OLSON (Farmer)
Adopted
Hazel SMITH (Mabel's best friend)
Jessie OLSON (8-yr-old daughter)
Julia OLSON (5-yr-old daughter)
David SMITH (Hazel's son)
Betsy SMITH (Hazel's daughter)
Sarah SMITH (Hazel's daughter)

BOOK FOUR: The Recollection 2013

See Family Tree Diagram in Book One

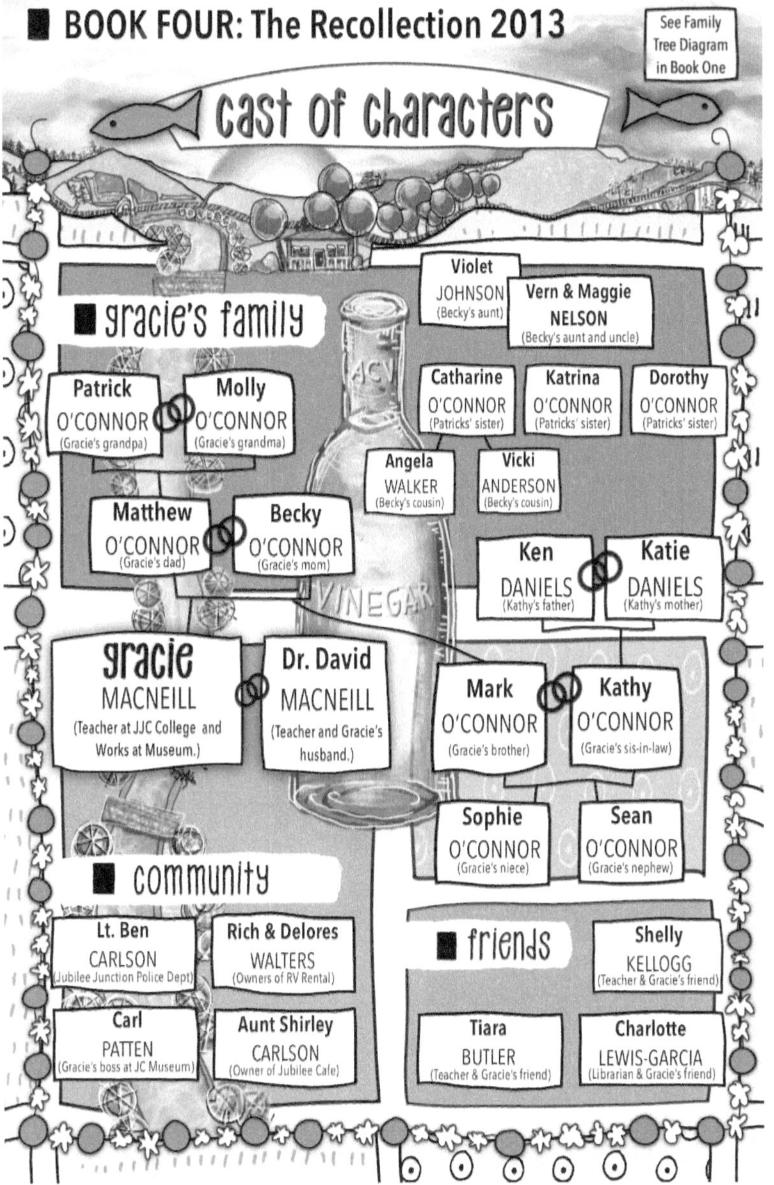

*M*y name is Gracie O'Connor MacNeill. Welcome to Jubilee Junction, Iowa. It's an old railroad town near the Jubilee River, founded by three families in the early 1850s. Many of those early settlers were Nelsons, Carlsons, or O'Connor's. My family has published the town's weekly paper, *The Jubilee Times*, since the 1850s. I spend one or two mornings a week there and the other three mornings at the local community college, where I teach writing and literature classes. Afternoons find me at the county museum arranging exhibits. I share a farmhouse with my husband David and our cat Agatha.

Yes, I know it sounds like a lot of work, but I enjoy it.

I'm named for my grandma, Grace Nelson Walters. She died three years ago, shortly after Grandpa Richard passed. I'm thankful for still having Great-Uncle Vern and Great-Aunts Maggie and Violet. Aunt Violet moved to a retirement community and gave me Grandma Grace's gift—a large wicker basket filled with a quilt, aprons, and two shoeboxes. One shoe box was full of cassettes with a tape recorder tucked underneath. Aunt Violet and I listened to the tapes together. Aunt Violet said that since I was the only granddaughter, Grandma Grace wanted to be sure I knew our family stories. On the tapes, Grandma Grace told the story of taking the train to California with her twin sisters during WWII.

Grandma Grace taught in a country school for two years before getting the letter from her cousin Ed urging the girls to join him in California. Grace and Vera got jobs at an aircraft factory producing B-17 bombers. Violet, a nurse, snagged a position at the San Diego Regional Naval Medical Center in Balboa Park. The girls lived in a boarding house, made friends, and attended a Methodist church made up of military families and others there to work on the home-front. Something terrible happened between the twins that shattered the family. The faded patchwork quilt my Grandma Grace called *the California quilt* on the tapes was the quilt she placed in the wicker basket. Hidden for sixty years in my great-grandma Ginny's bedroom, the quilt held the answer to the dispute.

As we listened to the tapes, Grandma revealed the secrets. She asked me to do what the family had failed to do 60 years earlier and talk about what happened in California. I was nervous, but my boyfriend David offered to be there to support me. Listening to Grandma Grace's story on the tapes helped Violet and Vera make up, and we figured out the mystery of *the California quilt*. My mom's cousin Donna finally heard the stories about her father, Don, who died before her birth.

Next, David and I investigated the origins of an antique red and green quilt. Grandma Molly found it in a relative's house forty years earlier. No one else wanted it, but there was a mysterious note wrapped inside the quilt. A rusted safety pin fastened a large lawyer's envelope to the quilt. Unfortunately, no one opened the envelope for several generations, and it went missing after a family dinner.

Grandma Molly wanted to know if the quilt dated back to the Civil War and who made it. David and I did research and learned it was an example of the Rustic Rose pattern and in remarkable condition. My great-great-grandfather, Michael O'Connor, and his best friend, James Nelson, fought in the Civil War with their younger brothers. They were part of the Iowa 24th Regiment.

Aunt Violet found an old telegram, and later a letter that provided clues. Charlotte, our town's librarian, found other documents, and we traced the movement of the 24th regiment with the help of the museum director, Carl, and David. Much later, we found letters and a journal that told the story. After a fierce battle near Winchester, Virginia, Michael, and a group of Union soldiers chased a group of Rebels and fighting broke out on the road. The Greycoats killed two of his soldiers and injured two others, so Michael and his men took refuge in a barn. The owner, a young widow named

Sarah, found them, and took the soldiers into her home, where she and a freed slave cared for the wounded men and gave them all food and water.

Sarah had just brought home three freed slaves from a nearby plantation with plans to take them to freedom. She and Michael made a deal. The soldiers would escort her group to Baltimore in exchange for her looking after the two injured soldiers and taking them home to Iowa. Along the way, they rescued two more slaves. Sarah and those five freed slaves traveled to Jubilee Junction, Iowa, to start new lives. She married Michael, becoming my great-great-great-grandmother. And as we got our answers, David proposed.

We got married at the Jubilee County Courthouse with plans for a renewal of vows ceremony in the fall. But there was no time to shop for wedding attire, so my mother called around asking my family for wedding dresses, and people loaned us a dozen lacey gowns. I chose one from the 1920s that my great-great-grandma Mary had worn—the same Grandma Mary who had kept the old quilt in her closet.

Learning about Michael and Sarah, Thomas and Rebecca gave us a rather unusual idea for our honeymoon, thanks to Uncle Rich offering to loan us one of his RVs. We drove cross-country and followed the path taken by my grandfather's regiment during the American Civil War.

On our first stop in St. Louis, my cousin Angela called. She wanted to bring me something. She showed up with her husband, some delicious BBQ, Grandma Mary's hope chest, and a new mystery. Inside the chest was a faded quilt, some letters, and a diary, hidden under a false bottom.

We learned Grandma Mary graduated from high school the year that the United States entered WWI. She was in love with a young man named Charlie. They got engaged before he left for France to fight during WWI, along with her older brother Bruce and his older brother Liam. Her mother, sister, and grandmother worked with her on a lovely Turkey Red and White Double Wedding Ring quilt for her hope chest. Unfortunately, Charlie died on the battlefield, a hero, plunging Mary into the depths of despair. Only when she received a letter from the young medic who was with Charlie when he died did she show any interest in life.

Mary returned to her daily routine of clerking at her father's general store. However, she dreaded any social gatherings and mourned for Charlie every night. Then the war ended, and her brother Bruce and Charlie's brother Liam came home. Liam had fallen in love with a young nurse named Jane, but she died of the Spanish flu. So he was grieving too. He and Mary became friends, sitting together at community gatherings and finding comfort in each other, friendship turned to love, and they married. She wore the lovely wedding dress I'd worn, a little satin shift with an overlay of lace.

Just as we got answers to questions about Grandma Mary's hope chest, Kathy gave birth to twins several weeks early, which is normal for twins. However, she needed a C-section and became anxious and cried every time she tried to lift the twins to nurse. Mark was worried and so were her mother and ours. Kathy's parents, Ken and Katie, moved in with them to help with the twins, Sophie and Sean. Kathy got support from family and friends and counseling for postpartum depression, but it took months for her to feel normal again.

At last it was time for our renewal of vows—and it was a lovely wedding. Our niece and nephew, as our flower girl and ring bearer, added their own sweet touches to the ceremony.

David and I moved out of my little rental house in town and into Mark and Kathy's old farmhouse this summer, and we're enjoying country life.

It's our first Christmas as a married couple and our first Christmas in our farmhouse. I've never decorated my house or had a Christmas tree because I always celebrated with my parents or my grandparents. Now I'm excited about creating holiday traditions with David.

Note: No cats were harmed in the writing of this story.

From Book Three
The Promise

"His mama and daddy always say, 'Use it up, wear it out, make it do, or do without.'"

~Marie

Mid-December 2013

       My iPhone chirped with a text from my sister-in-law, Kathy.

    `Got time to talk?`

I replied,

    `Sure, calling now.`

Kathy sounded flustered. "Gracie, you know how our moms are becoming such great friends? Mom went over to your mother's house yesterday and saw this old Crazy quilt draped over an antique bench. It made her remember seeing pictures of a Crazy quilt draped over a bench in some old photo album. This is going to sound crazy, but when she came home, she dug through a tub down in the storeroom and found her grandmother's photo album."

She took a breath. "Gracie, she has pictures of several Crazy quilts made by some little church sewing circle during the Depression. And she has a picture of your grandmother's quilt. Mom grew up in Peoria, Illinois, before moving here. How is that possible?"

My calm, smart sister-in-law was close to losing it.

"OK, Kathy. Sit down and take a few breaths. Does your mom still have that old photo album handy? I know what our old Crazy quilt looks like. I enjoyed looking at it as a child. It was at Great-Grandma Ginny's house, draped over that bench that held other old quilts. I'd love to see that photo."

"Mom wonders if you and David could figure this out. I know it's almost the holidays, but maybe after that you could investigate?" Kathy asked.

David walked back into the kitchen with a printout in his hand.

"Let me talk with David. I'm pretty sure we'll take the case because Grandma Grace loved Crazy quilts, and so do I. Talk to you later, Kathy. Send me that photo, okay?"

I glanced up at my beloved husband, who looked skeptical.

"Can't I leave you alone for five minutes without getting us involved with another quilt mystery? What is it this time?"

I explained it to him, and he thought about it. "What are the odds that two identical Crazy quilts would be out there in the world? How could someone who isn't from Jubilee Junction have a picture of your grandma's Crazy quilt? This is very intriguing."

I tore a sheet of paper from the underside of the notepad used to record menus and started a list. "I need to see Mom's quilt and compare it to this picture, research Depression-era quilts, talk to Aunt Violet, and see what Charlotte can find out for me in her archives."

David grinned as he picked up my mini clipboard, inspected my grocery list, and noted the aluminum foil and oranges.

He handed me the printout. "Here's the article about cats and how to keep them away from Christmas trees. Life is always interesting with you around, Gracie. I'm going to call Dad about those lights."

I scanned the article. It described how to use tin foil, orange peels, and apple cider vinegar to dissuade cats from tearing into Christmas trees and the gifts underneath.

David kissed me and walked away. "No more quilt mysteries while I'm gone. We have our hands full."

Agatha followed him. I wasn't jealous, but she spent a lot of time on that cat tree and wandering back and forth between our offices. She turned to follow David, looked back, and meowed quizzically at me. I laughed at myself. Sure, I was sharing David with my cat, but I was pretty sure I had the better part of the deal.

I picked up my new to-do list and headed upstairs. I had time to do research about the Great Depression, Crazy quilts, and quilting circles. This was going to be fun.

One

The Foreclosure
Edward

"The bank is something more than men, I tell you. It's the monster. Men made it, but they can't control it."

~John Steinbeck

Jubilee Junction Bank
April 1, 1933

Edward Richardson sat down behind his large oak desk at the Jubilee Junction bank. He'd shut his door before sitting down. He needed a minute to think. Edward reached into the bottom drawer for his bottle of whiskey and didn't bother with one of the two small glasses in the back of the drawer. The ache in his gut wasn't just the whiskey, or that he hadn't felt up to eating breakfast. The nameplate on his door proclaimed him the Bank President, but right now he would happily trade his job for the janitor's.

Edward picked up the piece of paper on his desk again and looked at it. It was a standard form, approving his branch bank in Prairie Falls to move forward on the foreclosure of his brother-in-law's farm. Edward needed to sign the document and send it off, setting into motion something he'd dreaded for months.

Samuel and his son Frank hadn't kept up with the payments on their mortgage of $2,000, still owing $1,000. His brother-in-law, Samuel, was a hard worker and an excellent farmer, but he had never been good with money even before the hard times hit.

It wasn't Samuel's fault that the price paid to the farmer for his products had collapsed. However, he bought a tractor and more sows instead of paying down the mortgage. Now he would lose it all to a farm auction, and so would his son.

Edward sighed, remembering his last conversation with Samuel, just two weeks before. He'd driven out to check on things and warn Samuel that he was in danger of losing the farm. Samuel was trying to raise money, but no one could afford to buy his tractor, and like most people, he was cash poor. Frank seemed more worried than his father, who leaned on the door to the barn as they talked. Frank listened to his uncle, gripping two buckets of feed for the pigs.

They'd seen three farms around them foreclosed on, and several forced farm sales. Their neighbors left in the middle of the night with all the possessions they could fit on a farm truck, abandoning the farm that had abandoned them.

Samuel had sighed. "Edward, you do your job. We'll be alright." He stood up and looked at Frank. "We better get back to work."

Edward remembered looking around the property and seeing the hard work Samuel and Frank had done over the years—and for what reward? To lose it all now? Why did he ever encourage Samuel to buy that blasted tractor anyway, instead of paying down the mortgage?

He took another slug of whiskey.

Edward picked up the newspaper with the latest farm report, and it was all bad news. The prices were at all-time lows with corn selling for eight cents a bushel, pork at three cents a pound, beef at five cents a pound, and eggs at ten cents a dozen. It cost more to plant a crop than farmers were getting for their harvest.

After a run on the banks in February, President Roosevelt declared a banking holiday. He shut down the banks nationwide March 6th through March 10th. The banking system had all but collapsed when people withdrew funds. Congress passed the Emergency Banking Act, and President Roosevelt gave a national radio address on March 12th. He reassured Americans that the Federal Reserve would ensure the funds in banks and only sound banks would open the next day. The public responded by returning more than half the funds they'd withdrawn. Jubilee Junction's Bank was deemed sound enough to reopen under FDIC protection if their loan portfolio met certain standards. Thank God for FDR's New Deal! Other banks weren't so lucky.

He put the newspaper down and cursed inwardly. *Blast it all!* The country was in a bad way, and all the smart people that let this happen should fix it. President Hoover hadn't been able to get the job done. He hoped the new president could do better, but it had been a terrible year so far. And now he had to foreclose on his own brother-in-law's farm.

How would Mabel react? She would be upset, no doubt. She would say he was heartless to turn out Samuel and her sister Edith and their son and his family. Frank and Marie were his niece and nephew, and they had those two little girls. How old were those girls, anyway? He searched his mind for Jessie and Julia's ages and guessed they were around five and seven. They were sweet little girls, with dark blonde hair and blue eyes, like their pretty mama. He reached for the whiskey again.

Edward had pondered paying off the loan himself. It would stretch him, but he couldn't manage it. He could swing $500 in cash, but the bank would still foreclose on the remaining debt of $500. Banks were desperate to comply with FDIC regulations. Dozens of banks in neighboring counties had already failed.

Just last week, the President of the Board said, "Richardson, do your job. We must hold on just a little longer. Surely the worst will pass us by, and the new administration in Washington, D. C. will help."

Edward had already foreclosed on thirty farms in the last six months. After he signed the first one, he felt such a heaviness in his gut that he could hardly breathe. That's when he snuck the whiskey bottle into his drawer.

He was a large man, in his late 50s, wearing an old suit, well pressed, with a clean shirt and tie. Mabel kept his hair trimmed. They lived in a spacious Queen Anne house on the corner of one of the finest streets in Jubilee Junction. He and Mabel were leading citizens, yet he could hardly hold up his head these days in church and on the street.

His hand was shaking as he signed his name on the form. He put the signed form into the envelope and got up from his chair. He grabbed a breath mint then opened the door, calling for his secretary, Mrs. Reed.

"Yes, Mr. Richardson?" She came to his door.

Without a word, he handed her the large envelope. She took it with a sigh, understanding. She had handled many such envelopes in the past few months.

"I'm going to lunch," he said, even though it was an hour and a half before noon. He had to talk to Mabel.

He walked home, shoulders sagging and gut aching.

Mabel was using a dust mop to clean the floors at home when he walked in, her hair up in a scarf. She glanced up, startled to see him so early. "I don't have your lunch ready."

"I'm not hungry." He sat down at the dining room table. "We need to talk."

"Oh no, Edward. What is it?"

"I signed off on the foreclosure papers on Samuel's farm. Edith, honey, I'm sorry. I thought I could raise the $1,000 to pay it off myself, but I came up short, and the bank would still foreclose."

Edith put down the dust mop and sat down, too. "What are they going to do? They worked so hard on that farm. Poor Samuel and Edith. Poor Frank, Marie, and those sweet little girls."

"I've been thinking. We have a big place here. They could stay with us until they get back on their feet. We have plenty of room, and there's the garden."

Mabel gazed at her husband and noticed the weariness etched on his face. It had been a hard year for everyone. Well, it'd been more than one hard year. Once Mabel had hired a cleaning woman to help, but when the cleaning woman's husband lost his job, they moved away. Mabel had been thinking about turning the place into a boarding house, but this might be better. She could help her family.

"I think that would be real nice. I don't know if Frank and Samuel could just sit around, but I would love to have those little girls here, and Edith and Marie. They could join my quilting circle."

Edward was too tired to snort. Leave it to Mabel to come up

with a bright side to the situation and think of her quilting circle. He was a lucky man, even if he felt like a failure who couldn't even save his own family from foreclosure. Edward felt so tired. He put his head down on his arms on the table.

Mabel put her hands on Edward's shoulders and tried to comfort him. "I'm not angry, dear. We'll do what we can to help them. That's what family does, after all. Let me get you some coffee and toast. You left the house without breakfast this morning."

Edward sat back up and wiped his eyes, hearing Mabel bustle around in the kitchen. He'd done something right with his life when he married Mabel. She always knew what to say, and she had faith that things would work out for the good.

Once, not so long ago, Edward had considered himself a man of faith. But he wasn't his old self, confident and optimistic before the foreclosures. It took something out of a man to sign those bank forms, knowing what was going to happen to those farm families and their rural communities. He hadn't been able to save them. However, he had to come up with a plan to help Frank and Samuel and their families.

Two

The Mystery Unfolds
Gracie

"Give a woman some scraps of fabric, needle and thread, and a couple of friends around a big table, and you'll see yourself a quilt coming together."

~Grandma Virginia Nelson (Ginny)

Ten days before Christmas

After I got off the phone with Kathy and settled at the computer in my attic office, I called my mom. I'd just opened a browser and was typing in *Depression-era Crazy quilts* when she answered.

"So, what happened with Katie?" I asked. "Kathy just called. Tell me everything."

I put the phone on speaker and set it on a little stand. I grabbed a notepad and three freshly sharpened pencils.

Mom told me about asking Katie for tea for a brief respite from the twins. The grandfathers shooed them off, telling them to have fun for the afternoon. Matthew and Ken played with the twins in the living room while Kathy napped and Mark did chores. So, they left.

"We drove to our house and walked in the front door, chatting. Katie and I have so much in common. It's been wonderful getting to know her and Ken better." Mom paused, trying to remember every detail. "Remember, I've got your great-grandpa's old quilt chest in the hallway with the Crazy quilt draped on it. As we walked in, Katie stopped, stared, and turned to me. I wasn't sure what was going on.

"Katie said, 'I've seen this quilt. I've seen this bench,' and then she paused. 'How is that possible? My mother has an old photo album, and that's where I saw the photo. Seeing it sparked the memory. I've looked at pictures of this quilt my whole life, Becky.'"

Mom was emotional as she described the scene, and I felt a tingle up my spine. *What was going on here?*

Mom continued, "I was astonished, as you might imagine. Katie asked me for permission to examine the quilt. I brought her a dining room chair and one for me, and we sat and inspected it, turning it over to see the stitching on the back."

"'It's lovely,' Katie said, finally, her voice trembling with excitement."

Mom remembered the conversation. "Yes, I agree. My Grandma Ginny told me stories about these Crazy quilts. They were made during the Great Depression from the scraps left over from other sewing projects—from aprons and dresses. Women used to have an old pillowcase that held their scrap collection, and it was precious to them. Grandma Ginny used to say, 'Give a woman some scraps of fabric, needle and thread, and a couple of friends, and you'll get yourself a quilt.'"

Mom paused, then said, "Katie smiled when I said that, but seemed sad. I opened Grandpa's chest and showed her a few of the other quilts our family made. She admired them all, especially that pink Double Wedding Ring. But I could tell that she was fixated on that Crazy quilt.

"We had our tea and brownies, we took some photos, and then we headed back to the kids' farmhouse—with the quilt. We folded it up and wrapped it up in a sheet—just the way you like it—and put it into a tub.

"Once there, we walked down to the basement storeroom and found Katie's tub with photo albums and such. Katie dug into it, and came up triumphant with an old photo album. She found the page and showed it to me. I thought my heart would stop, Gracie. It *was* the same quilt and bench."

Mom paused; her voice had become shaky with emotion. My

mother was seldom flustered. She had a Zen-like superpower for staying calm, and it had gotten us out of a few dilemmas, so this got my full attention. Most recently, when our second wedding—a renewal of vows—almost had to be canceled, she found another venue within half an hour. Mom could persuade people to do things they knew they should do but resisted. She didn't get rattled—until now.

I had a dozen questions. "Wow, Mom. I understand why Kathy and Katie were so surprised. That's strange. Didn't Katie talk about growing up in Peoria before moving to Iowa? When can I see these photos?"

I stood up, restless, already moving towards the stairs.

"I'm over here at Mark and Kathy's. Why don't you come see for yourself? You're going to want to borrow the album to scan in the picture. I didn't think you'd want me to take a picture of the photo with my phone."

I said I'd be right over and said goodbye. Once downstairs, I slipped on my short boots and grabbed my keys before I dropped my phone into my purse. I stopped to add a warm hooded sweatshirt, then put on my winter coat and walked outside, looking for David, who was out in the garage.

He'd bought a small heater for his workshop area and a cozy wooden chair with a padded seat. David sat reading *Popular Mechanics* to learn how to build sawhorses. He glanced up and smiled. Fortunately, Mark had installed several shop lights, so there was plenty of light.

"I'm heading over to Kathy's to see the photo album with pictures of my great-grandma's Crazy quilt. Want to come? Mom was freaked out just now, telling me the story of Katie looking at the Crazy quilt on the antique bench."

David's eyebrows raised, and he put down the magazine. "Sure, I'm curious. I've never seen your mom even a little freaked out."

He turned off the heater, unplugged it, and slipped on his jacket.

We took his SUV and arrived just a few minutes later, since it was only a mile away.

We knocked and waited at the kitchen door, where Mom and

Katie greeted us, along with Chewie and Han Solo, Ken's two Golden Retrievers. After sniffing us and accepting a few pats, the dogs settled down beside the grandfathers. Ken held Sean and Dad held Sophie at the dining room table. There was a sense of expectancy in the room.

The Moms, as Mark and Kathy were referring to our mom and hers, bustled about and brought us coffee and tea. We took off our coats and hung them on hooks near the back door.

"Thanks for coming over," Katie said.

Mom nodded, and I saw her face—flushed with excitement, eyes brimming with tears. I couldn't recall many times Becky O'Connor had been at a loss for words. Make that any time.

David and I sat down at the dining room table where an old photo album sat open. After a few sips, I put my tea aside and glanced at Katie.

"Yes, please look, Gracie," she said.

I took a pair of thin cotton gloves out of my purse and slipped them on.

Katie sat opposite me, watching intently.

I picked up the photo album and asked for a tea towel, which Mom had already fetched and passed over.

By now, Kathy, Katie, Mom, Mark, David, and the grandfathers—each holding a twin—were watching me. The dogs stood up and whined.

I usually worked alone in my basement workroom at the museum. This seemed more like a command performance. I felt a little self-conscious, as if I should ask David for a scalpel and maybe to wipe my sweaty brow. I resisted the urge to giggle, thinking, *What's the deal with Mom? What could be in this old photo album to have six grown adults acting so weird?*

As I picked up the photo album and placed it on the tea towel, it fell open to a page. *Whoa!* I immediately saw the cause for excitement. "Check this out, David. It is *the* Crazy quilt and Grandma's old bench." My mouth went dry as I craved a Diet Dr Pepper instead of the Constant Comment in my cup.

I gazed again at the photograph of my grandmother's antique

bench with the Crazy quilt laid out on top. *How is this possible?* I slid it out and turned it over. It was blank on the back. Not surprising, but disappointing.

I ignored everyone and took a few minutes to go through the album, turning pages and evaluating the photos.

At last I glanced back up and everyone was staring at me—even the babies it seemed. Chewie and Han Solo stood on either side of Ken, trying to figure out why their humans were acting so strangely. Chewie whined.

The Moms stared at me even more intently.

"Can I take this to the museum tomorrow and scan all these pictures?" I asked.

Katie said, "Yes, certainly. I know you'll take care of it. What do you think?"

I glanced at David, hesitating. My thoughts were swirling. I understood my mom's sudden quietude.

He stared back and jumped in. "Gracie's hooked. This is a quilt mystery alright. What are the odds of two identical quilts and two identical benches?"

David turned to Katie. "What do you know about your family? Did they ever pass through Iowa—and Jubilee Junction in particular?"

He took a sip of coffee.

Katie shook her head in bewilderment. "I grew up in Illinois. Mom was from Peoria, or at least that's what I thought. She didn't talk about her family history, and my father said not to push her. I have three quilts, and this album, and an old blue enamel turkey roaster, and that's about it."

Several people nodded sympathetically.

They all looked at me, waiting, Mom still silent.

Mark jumped in, "C'mon, Gracie. Help us out here, sis. What's up with the photo of the old Crazy quilt?"

Three

The Photo Album
Gracie

"No one can possibly have lived through the Great Depression without being scarred by it. No amount of experience since the Depression can convince someone who has lived through it that the world is safe economically."

~Isaac Asimov

I turned back two pages, sighed, and rotated the photo album. I wanted them to see the picture that left me gobsmacked and unable to say anything a moment before. Everyone leaned forward.

I pointed at a group of women gathered around a large quilting frame. "Do you recognize anyone here?" I slid the tea towel towards Mom.

She examined the photo, using the tea towel to hold up the album.

"That's Grandma Ginny!" Mom replied in amazement. She stared around the room, her eyes shining with excitement.

Kathy stared at her mother, who stood up and then sat back down in her chair and put her hands on her face, thinking.

Katie was astonished. "I don't understand. I've looked at those pictures for years and assumed they were from a group in Peoria. How could my mother have been here in Jubilee Junction? And apparently, she knew your grandmother?"

I reclaimed the photo album and rotated it, turning the pages. "There are at least four other photos here that have familiar landmarks or people in them. I'd like to scan the entire photo album with your consent. I can create a Google Photos album and share it with you or burn them onto a DVD or flash drive for you if you'd like."

"Yes, please." Katie nodded.

I grabbed my notebook. "Tell me your mother's name, Katie."

"Of course. Jessica Harper. My father's name is James Harper. And my grandparents were Marie and Frank Olson. My great-grandparents were Samuel and Edith Olson."

Mom stood up and retrieved the quilt from the sideboard. It was wrapped in a sheet, and she handled it reverently as she placed it on the dining room table. The Moms and I examined it, rotating it and turning it over. It was lovely, filled with tiny irregular shapes: bright purples, oranges, blues, and yellows, with a few whites and blacks. A mix of plain fabric, prints, plaids, and florals. A myriad of scraps placed here and there to comprise the whole. It was the quilt in the photo.

Dad stood behind me, carrying Sophie. He bent down to take a closer look. "You have a new puzzle to solve, Gracie," he commented.

Sophie reached out towards the quilt, fascinated with the colors.

"I'll take the quilt into the museum and lay it out for a few photos as well," I said as I wrapped the photo album in the tea towel and placed it down in the tub with the quilt.

The spell was broken. Everyone went back to whatever they were doing. But there was a buzz of excitement. Katie and Mom moved towards the kitchen, and Kathy sat on the floor, next to a large laundry basket, folding onesies on the coffee table, looking thoughtful.

I jotted down some notes about those photos and put the notebook back in my purse. I opened my arms for Sophie, who came to me with a smile. Ken handed over Sean to David, and we played with the babies for half an hour while the dogs walked around us.

The twins were rolling over, trying to crawl, and liked to sit up in their Bumbo chairs, funny little foam chairs that support young babies. David and I put the babies down on the carpet and crawled around while the babies stared back at us and made noises.

Sophie scooted backwards, and Sean tried to imitate her, going forward. Then Sophie rolled over, and so did Sean, bumping into her. Sophie began to cry, probably more startled than hurt. I picked her up to comfort her, and she grabbed my curls with one little fist.

David grabbed a small toy and offered it to Sophie, and she let go. I'd started tearing up. "Ow. This kid has a firm grip."

Katie and Mom chatted while they got out plates, forks, and cinnamon rolls. More coffee and tea got poured, so we visited with the adults again.

An hour passed, and we headed home. I assured them I would get to work on figuring out the puzzle.

Mark walked us out, while David carried the tub. When we reached our car, Mark thanked me. He's fond of his in-laws and they've been invaluable, helping with the twins. They'd rented out their house and moved in before the twins' arrival. Ken had taken a leave of absence from his marketing company, and Katie had taken early retirement from her teaching career.

Mark opened the back hatch, and David put the tub inside.

"I've never seen Katie like this before, and Kathy hasn't either. And, of course, it's spooky seeing Mom speechless. Thanks for checking it out. I know you two will figure it out." Mark tried to grin.

I nodded, and so did David. It was snowing, light little flakes at first, with a promise of heavier snow later.

"There's a story here, Mark, and we'll find it," I promised him as David shut the hatch.

Mark waved, and we headed home.

David pulled into our garage. We walked the short distance to our back door, David carrying the tub with the quilt and photo album. He put it down in the dining room and smiled at me. "Is this spot okay?"

I nodded. Mom had found the lid for the container, so its contents were safe from Agatha.

He checked the clock. "I'm going back to the garage for a few minutes to put together my list for Menards."

"Sounds good," I agreed, already taking the stairs to the second floor and then my office. I couldn't wait to sort out this puzzle. *What brought Katie's mother to Jubilee Junction, and why didn't she talk about it with her daughters?*

Four

Moving Out Day
Marie

"Sometimes you gotta hold on to your faith, when you lose everything else."

~Marie Olson

April 10, 1933

$\mathcal{I}$ straighten from packing pots and pans in the barrel and rub my aching back then pat my forehead. I'd put a thin cotton scarf on my head this morning to keep the hair out of my face as I worked, but that was hours ago. I take it off, run my fingers through my hair, and readjust the scarf.

Walking back into our bedroom, I pass the mirror. Staring at the reflection, I behold a thin woman with dark blonde wavy hair and deep blue eyes wearing a faded, flour-sack house dress, an old sweater, and a shabby apron. I reach my hand out toward her. "You look old," I tell her. "So much older than my thirty-two years. The past decade has done that."

"Mama, Jessie said I can't take my teddy bear because it won't fit in the suitcase." Five-year-old Julia stomped in clutching her beloved teddy bear.

I sigh. "Can you just carry it, then? Go help your sister."

"Yes, Mama," the little girl walks away, triumphant.

We were packing everything we own in a farm truck. Frank had built a framework onto it so that it looks like a covered truck now, with tarps fastened onto 2 x 4s. I've sorted things to fit into four trunks and two wooden barrels. We have two battered suitcases filled with clothing. The farm sale took the larger pieces of furniture, not that those pieces would fit in the truck, anyway, but it still hurts. I'm taking blankets and quilts, pillows, four chairs, and Grandma's round, drop-leaf table, a small box of books from my preacher father, a small chest of drawers, our clothes, pots and pans, and a small bookcase. The barrel is almost full, but there's room for Grandma's battered tin mixing bowl and utensils. I add my pillowcase of scraps and sewing kit and put on the lid.

I already packed a box of home canned goods wrapped in newspaper. The flour, sugar, and coffee canisters fit into another box. I wrap our dishes in sheets of newspaper in the first barrel and add old scrunched up newspaper and towels around them. My washtub holds the cleaning products—baking soda, sponges, washcloths, vinegar, soap flakes, and a scrub board. I slide the cleaning things into a faded old pillowcase and put it back in the washtub.

The little girls collected their toys and books and put them into a small box. I check on them and praise them for their help. They've packed up their things, and the room is almost bare. The bank sale took our beds, our couch, and Mama's piano. I take down the curtains, thinking, *I won't leave anything behind. After all, I can always cut them up for a quilt.* I check the closet and notice something up on the very top shelf.

Mama's old jewelry box! I put it up here years ago and forgot about it.

I stand on tiptoe to be sure nothing else is there. I clutch the jewelry box to my chest, suddenly in tears, and put it into my suitcase after tying an old scrap of fabric around it to be sure it doesn't come open. I wipe my tears on my apron and tell the girls to check every room and let me know if there are any curtains still hanging.

"Yes Mama," Julia says. At eight, she's my little helper.

I walk back into our bedroom, taking down the curtains and checking the closet shelf one more time. It is empty. The bed was gone, and so was the dresser. In the living room are four folding cots which will serve as our new couch and beds, already folded up, and ready to go out to the truck.

Frank walks into the house and look around. Wearing overalls with a thick sweatshirt and his heavy boots, he's a tall, thin man, thirty-two, handsome with dark eyes, dark hair, and the weight of the world creasing his face. But he's a good man. He walks up to me from behind, puts his arms around me, and says, "You've worked hard here, Marie. We're almost done. Better days are ahead, like my ma says."

He lets out a deep sigh and tears himself away from me, then rolls a loaded barrel out to the truck where he's left a space. I follow with several blankets and pillows, fitting them in wherever they can go. The little girls put on their thick sweaters and run out with their box of toys, and their papa finds a space. He returns for the cots and wedges them in so they won't fall out, then goes back in to get the suitcases.

I walk back inside the house for one last look, and the girls followed me, not knowing what else to do. I smile and hug them. "What's left?"

Julia says, "Mama, you forgot the kitchen curtains. Let me get them."

I lift Julia up to the kitchen counter and together we take the curtains down. I hand them to Jessie. Then Julia says, "Mama, there's a book on top of the icebox. I think I can reach it."

She hands it to me.

Mama's cookbook!

"Julia, good girl. Can you see anything else?" I ask, remembering how I searched for a recipe and gave up when I didn't have most of the ingredients. I left the book up there a week or two ago.

"No, Mama."

I wrap the book in the curtains and tuck it into the last box in the corner.

"I want to help, too, Mama," says Jessie.

"Alright then, please check under that sink and in the corners for Mama."

We check all the drawers in the kitchen. Jessie peeks under the sink, squealing when she spies a sponge and a box of baking soda. This, too, gets wrapped up and placed in the box.

We examine the bathroom next, but the curtains are gone, and the towels are already packed around the dishes. There is just a little bar of soap in the tub, worn to a sliver with use. I take it anyway. *Waste not, want not.*

I wander through the house looking wistfully at the small, dingy rooms. We've lived here for eight years. It is the only home our girls have ever known. I always thought it a cheery, homey place when it was filled with furniture and laughter. Perhaps it has always been a sad and dingy place. After all, it's just the tenant's house on my father-in-law's farm. The bank's farm, now.

We walk out together, the girls and I. I carry the box. I find my pillowcase that holds the cleaning things and add the bar of soap. There was nothing left to pack in the house.

Five

Packing up Papa's Truck
Marie

"The Great Depression in the United States was caused—I won't say caused—was enormously intensified and made far worse than it would have been by bad monetary policy."
~Milton Friedman

Frank's out in his shop, a room off the garage, packing a small box with four coffee cans of screws, nails, and other small hardware as we enter.

"Hi Daddy. Can we help?" Julia asks.

"Sure thing. Here take Daddy's overalls and roll them up. Mama can help."

"I want to help, too!" Jessie looks around.

"Of course," he replies.

Frank and I look around the small space with the built-in workbench he loved and a heater in the corner that burned corn cobs. It's almost empty. He sees a small folding step stool and some scraps of oak used to build the workbench. He ties the wood together with a piece of twine and hands it to Jessie.

"Find a place for Papa's wood, Jessie Girl?"

Frank grabs the step stool and leads us out to the truck.

She and Julia peek into the truck, with me holding little Jessie up. "There!" She points to a good spot. He takes the rolled-up overalls from Julia and finds a place for them as well as the step stool. His truck is full. Then Frank sighs, takes his cap off and runs his hand on top of his head. He has one of his headaches, I can tell, but he doesn't complain

26

"Girls, let's take one more look inside and say goodbye to the house. Leave that teddy bear here, Jessie Girl. We'll be right back," Frank says.

We walk through the house, holding hands, not saying much. Jessie tells him they found grandma's cookbook up on the cupboard and Mama's old jewelry box in their bedroom closet. He nods.

He checks all the tall shelves, opens closets, finds nothing, and turns back.

"You girls done a fine job here of clearing us out. Let's go visit Grandpa and Grandma Olson, shall we?"

We put on our coats, walk out the door, close it, glance at each other, and he kisses me. "Better days," he whispers.

Frank opens the passenger side door and lifts little Jessie up. Julia climbs up by herself, and Frank takes my hand to help me step up. He starts the engine, moves forward, stops, adjusts the load, and finds one more piece of rope to support the two cots. Then we head off, driving down the familiar little dirt road, not looking back.

I remember just three weeks earlier when Samuel and Edith came to visit one night. The girls were in bed. We sat around the kitchen table as Samuel told us he was sorry and showed us the letter from the bank. He'd fallen behind on the mortgage payments and the bank was going to foreclose on the farm. They'd lost the land we'd all worked on for almost 20 years.

Edward choked up, "I'm sorry. We promised you two the farm would be yours one day."

Edith and I had a good cry while the men looked on uncomfortably and Edward blew his nose.

The following week, the neighborhood gathered, and the auctioneer sold the animals, the tractor, and other equipment. Edith and I cried when the farm sale was over, and our neighbors tried to comfort us. But everyone is worried. Times are bad for farmers. Between low prices for crops, land prices dropping, and being cash poor, many farmers struggle to pay the mortgage. Truth be told, times aren't so good for banks, either. Many are failing across the Midwest. No wonder people are saving nickels and dimes in coffee cans under the bed.

Edith confided in me she never thought her own brother-in-law would foreclose on them. She trusted Edward Richardson when he said buying that new tractor was a wise investment two years ago. He'd said the same thing when they'd expanded their swine operation a few years before that. Of course, she'd also trusted Samuel to keep up with the payments, but she couldn't bear to blame him. Their excellent investments had ruined them, and they had nothing to show for twenty years of farming this good Iowa farmland.

That didn't matter now, because tomorrow, we were getting up and driving off in our two trucks. Thank goodness Samuel and Frank were so handy because we wouldn't be homeless. Samuel had hung onto their big farm truck.

He and Edith had driven to visit some family in California several years ago, and Samuel had an idea. He and Frank added a wooden frame, which became a tiny house, about 8 1/2 feet wide and 18 feet long, with a door on the side.

The men built a large wooden chest with a hinged lid for supplies. Samuel and Edith slept in two cots, folded up during the day.

Samuel and Edith had fun driving out West, and the truck house was quite the attention-getter. Whenever they'd stopped for gas and food, people wanted a peek inside. She was proud to show it off. But she never imagined it would be their only home.

The men kept working on the truck house after the foreclosure. Now, as you entered through the side door, there was a countertop to prepare food, with a cupboard above. Below was an icebox and portable stove to cook food outside. Samuel and Frank built a narrow counter next to the door with a cupboard above for storage. The counter had two drawers for cooking supplies. Edith filled the cupboards with spices, and her canisters of sugar, coffee, tea, and flour.

Frank and Samuel built four narrow benches with storage below for blankets and pillows. Above, Frank added four long narrow tables that could swing up or down and fit on the wall when not in use, thanks to the hooks that held them in place.

At the other end of the truck house was a bunk bed built into the over-the-cab space with plenty of room for the two little girls. Edith arranged two pallets, with several pillows and blankets for each little girl. Two trunks filled the space below with a small space to pass through to the cab. It would be tight, but we'd manage.

Frank devised a clever little rope and metal ladder that slid under the mattress. The girls showed me how they'd climb on top of the flat trunks and then use the ladder to get into their beds.

The girls loved the bunk, and Frank and I and his folks had a place to sleep.

We'd manage, alright. After all, Frank's ma assured me that God was faithful and better times were just ahead. Weren't they?

Six

The Search Begins
Gracie

"The beauty in a Crazy quilt comes from the creativity of the women who could take scraps of fabric and arrange them in such a pleasing way."

~Charlotte Lewis-Garcia.

The next day, I carried the tub into the Jubilee library. Charlotte wanted to compare the quilt with the pictures. She also offered me the use of her high-resolution scanner. I sent her a text telling her we had a new quilt mystery.

Charlotte was ready for me. She draped a sheet on a large table in her workroom. I set the tub down and retrieved the photo album. Charlotte donned a pair of cotton gloves. She sighed when she caught sight of the quilt.

We leafed through the album. I'd made a detailed inventory last night, with help from my mother and Katie. We'd show the pictures to Aunt Violet, of course, because a couple of them included people we didn't know. So far, I'd spotted half a dozen pictures that were taken in Jubilee Junction, including the Jubilee Methodist Church, for one. There were pictures of the church quilting circle, and so far, three Jubilee Junction women had been identified. There was a beautiful Queen Anne house that resembled the one over on Second Street. In one photo, a huge farm truck with what looked like a small house built on it was in the vacant lot next to the Queen Anne. We scanned the album, labeled the pictures, and copied them onto two flash drives—one for me and one for Katie.

Next, we unfolded the quilt, laid it out on the sheet, and admired it again. I got out my Canon EOS and began taking photos.

Charlotte smiled. "This is just gorgeous. I'm looking at all these pieces and wondering at the hours it must have taken to lay it out and put it all together."

We turned over the quilt and repeated the process of documenting the quilt by taking pictures.

"The beauty in a Crazy quilt comes from the creativity of the women who could take scraps of fabric and arrange them in such a pleasing way." Charlotte stared up at me. "This is a story worth discovering and sharing, Gracie."

I noticed something that I'd never remembered seeing before. Or maybe I'd never paid attention to these details before. I squinted at the border. There was something else there—a date?

We used a magnifying glass and there it was: "Loaves N Fishes, 1933."

Only it was the symbols of two little loaves of bread plus the N and three fish and 1933.

Charlotte and I stared at each other, and there was a new gleam of interest in her eye. "What's that about?"

I shrugged, feeling stumped. "It's a reference to the story of feeding the 5,000 in the Bible, but what does that have to do with quilts?"

Charlotte used the whiteboard on the wall to record what we knew, suspected, or needed to find out.

Katie's Grandma's album was undated, but the note on the quilt's border included 1933.

Check out ownership of the Queen Anne house on Second Street in 1933.

Check the records of the Jubilee Junction Methodist church for the identities of the others in the quilting circle pictures.

Gracie's Great-Grandmother Virginia (Ginny) Grace Nelson was a member of the quilting club and took two of her daughters along, Grace and Violet.

Young Grace and Violet appeared to be maybe 7 and 9 years old in the pictures.

Who were the two visiting women? Older and younger, maybe mother and daughter? Two little girls?

Check for information about the message on the border of the quilt. What do the symbols mean? What do loaves and fishes have to do with quilts?

We sat down in her office to use the library's genealogy databases, starting with Ancestry, but we didn't get far. I'd written Katie's parents' names on her mother's side and ran into dead ends when trying to create her family tree. I tried using the names she'd given me for her father's side and got a little further. We didn't have middle names, birthplaces or dates for her grandparents.

Grabbing my iPhone, I called Katie. "Katie, is there anyone who would know more about your mother's side of the family? I need middle initials, birthdates, if we're going to find any information. Any aunts and uncles, nephews, or cousins who were into family history?"

She thought. "I'll call my cousin in Peoria." Twenty minutes later, she called back in tears. "The people who could answer my questions have been dead for twenty years. My cousin was just as frustrated as I am. She said her mother never talked about her past that much."

"Don't worry, we have some other ideas," I said.

Charlotte looked thoughtful as I said goodbye to Katie. "We haven't checked census records or the city directories."

I was due at the college to give my last final exam in half an hour. I left the tub there in her care, telling her I'd be back to pick it up.

As I walked out, I said, "We'll think of something, okay? We aren't giving up."

Charlotte folded the quilt back up, still wearing the cotton gloves. "Of course not. Who said anything about giving up?"

I gave the final and then walked back to the office, where Shelly sat grading papers and Tiara was using the computer to enter grades in her gradebook.

Shelly glanced over. "What's going on, Gracie? I can tell something's up."

Tiara turned around. "What now?"

So I shared my story about the Crazy quilt, the photo album, and the mystery.

Shelly responded, "Depression-era Crazy quilts? I love Crazy quilts."

I got out my phone and showed them the photos I'd taken at the library.

"Beautiful," Tiara said. "All those teeny scraps. It's like artwork."

Shelly held my phone and moved to the next picture, the whiteboard, with a list of things to discover. "Loaves and fishes?" She asked. "What's that about?"

I shrugged. "I don't know beyond the obvious—the Bible story. I hope to figure it out."

Shelly smiled. "You will."

Tiara nodded, glancing away from her computer screen.

We chatted about our holiday plans as we graded or checked our college email.

Tiara's two daughters were coming home with their boyfriends, and they were going to meet Mama's new boyfriend, Doctor Terry. She anticipated spending time with them all. "I want to drive around and admire the lights, watch our favorite holiday movies, and play board games." She sighed. "Of course, if there's an emergency, Terry will leave to attend to his patients. He's a wonderful doctor."

Tiara's church was having a Christmas Eve service and hosting a potluck afterward. Tiara included her Aunt Phoebe and cousin Jerome in her plans. Aunt Phoebe had known Tiara all her life and was her grandmother's best friend. Now that Grandma was gone, Aunt Phoebe was there and so was Jerome, who was still single.

Shelly's family was headed to the paternal grandparents' in Des Moines. "We'll probably fit in some sledding, build a snowman, go visit Santa at the mall, and drive around and see the lights. His family is wonderful—a sister and brother live there, and both have children. So it will be a madhouse with seven cousins between the ages of one and ten. The grandparents have a large basement with a guest room, family room, and bathroom, so there's plenty of room for us. We'll eat too many cookies, drink too much cocoa, and wear crazy look-alike pajamas. But the kids will have fun playing with their cousins, so I'm looking forward to it."

She grabbed my phone and stared at the quilt. "Gracie, I've seen some of those fabrics in a quilt my grandma kept that her mother made from old flour and feed sacks. During the Great Depression, women needed fabric to make clothes for their families. Companies began printing feed sacks and flour sacks in bright colors and patterns."

I regarded my friend with respect. "Thanks, Shelly! I'll check that out."

Tiara was packing up her messenger bag. "I have some kitchen towels from my grandma, and she always called them flour sack towels. They're made from soft cotton perfect for drying dishes. Now I'm curious."

I got out my notebook and jotted a note. *Flour sack towels. Feed sacks for fabric.* Then I sent a text message to Charlotte.

> *Check out flour sacks from the depression era. Shelly recognized several patches in the Crazy quilt.*

I packed up for the day and headed for the library.

Charlotte had moved to the front desk and opened the library. A few patrons were browsing the DVD rack and *New Titles* displays. She checked out a young mom and her toddler getting a stack of picture books. Then she turned to me with a smile. "I found something. Shelly was right!" She gestured to her computer screen, and I glanced over her shoulder to see an article about Gingham Girl flour sacks.

"One hundred pounds of flour?" I repeated to myself. "It took two or three sacks from 100-pound bags of flour to make a dress for a woman. That's a lot of bread to bake."

"I sent you the link. Remember, they baked bread every day in those days. There are lots of references to flour sack dish towels and clothing," Charlotte said. Then she turned to help a library patron.

"Thank you again, Charlotte. I'll let you know what I find." I picked up the tub and headed for the door.

I was still pondering 100-pound sacks of flour when I walked into the house, balancing my messenger bag on top of the large tub. My phone was in my pocket, and my purse hiked up on my shoulder.

I set things down, said hello to the cat, grabbed my purse and messenger bag, and headed for the stairs to my office.

Once I got there, I turned on my laptop and began searching for the depression era and flour and feed sacks. I was scribbling notes when my phone rang. It was my mother.

"How are you doing, Gracie?" Mom asked.

I told her about the research on Depression-era flour sack towels, and she listened quietly. Then she said, "Uncle Vern has been visiting Jimmy Joe. He's been despondent and finally poured out his story after half a dozen visits. Billy's mother did not leave him. She died—the victim of domestic violence. She hid the bruises at first. But then Darlene became pregnant with Billy, and the beatings continued. Shirley, Jimmy Joe's wife, confronted her son and demanded he get help for his drinking and anger. But Jimmy Joe was reluctant to interfere in his son's marriage.

When Billy was two, his mother tried to leave and take Billy. James was drunk, and Darlene called Shirley for help. She and Jimmy Joe drove to the house where they found their daughter-in-law in tears and their grandson screaming. James Junior had picked him up in anger when the little boy tugged on his father's pant leg, trying to stop him from hurting his mother.

"No hit! No hit!" the little boy screamed.

Jimmy Joe walked in, saw the situation and got between his son and his daughter-in-law and grandson. Shirley took Billy by the hand. "Let's go in the other room and let Daddy talk to Grandpa." She looked at Darlene and put her arm around her. "We'll get you fixed up."

The two men stood at the entrance to the living room. Pillows and toys scattered around, an end table toppled over, and half a dozen empty beer cans were by the couch.

Jimmy Joe picked them up and put them on the coffee table. He turned to his son. "You gotta stop this drinking, James, because you got a good woman and a sweet little boy. You're a grown man, Son, and you got responsibilities. What's wrong with you?" demanded Jimmy Joe.

He picked up the end table, putting it back in place. His son sat down heavily. He shrugged. "She's always fussing over that boy. She didn't have supper on the table when I came home."

"Darlene is that boy's mama. It's her job to fuss over him. I didn't raise you to beat your wife or get drunk every night. You show her respect, you hear me? Your mama is beside herself—she's so upset. I'm going to ask the pastor to stop by and talk to you." Jimmy Joe looked at his son and spoke firmly. "What's going on? You never used to be like this."

James exhaled. "I'm sorry, Pa. Sometimes I just get so angry and it's like I don't know I've hit her again. I love her, I do, and I don't want to lose her."

"Well, something's gotta change. I see that pile of empty beer cans outback on the porch. You're drinking too much, and when you're drunk, you're more likely to get riled up. Your mama is looking after Darlene. Let's go out to the kitchen and find some coffee." His father gestured to the kitchen, where Shirley had already started a pot of coffee and had a casserole in the oven.

Darlene was sitting at the kitchen table, drinking some tea. Her hand shook when James entered the room. Her cheek was swollen, and bruises were evident on her upper arm and face. The little boy sat on her lap eating animal crackers. He looked up at his father fearfully. "No hit?" he asked.

Shirley looked at her husband, fire in her eyes. She spoke in silence. "No more hitting, Billy. Right, son? You got something to say to your wife and child?"

James exhaled. "Darlene, I'm sorry. Baby, you know I love you. I'm sorry, Billy, no hitting." He sat down at the table and drank the coffee. Darlene was silent.

After the family ate supper, Grandma Shirley tucked Billy into bed. The four adults sat in the living room, now restored to order. James Junior promised his parents he wouldn't drink. His father looked around, found a couple of six packs on the back porch and put them by the front door. He sat down and talked to his son in a lowered voice and James nodded several times.

Shirley took her daughter-in-law aside. She hugged Darlene

and whispered, "I don't care if he's my son. I'm ashamed of him, and I'm worried about you. You lock yourself in the bathroom if he drinks again, and you take Billy and the phone with you."

Things seemed to be going well. Then, a few weeks later, the police called Jimmy Joe in the middle of the night, and they went back to the house, where their beautiful daughter-in-law Darlene Mae had been beaten again, sustaining head injuries. When they arrived, there was a squad car outside and several police officers were inside, gathering evidence. A neighbor was watching the little boy, who was confused, and asking for Mama.

Jimmy Joe and Shirley found a duffle bag and packed things for Billy and took him home. Their son had been arrested and taken to jail.

Later that day, Shirley went up to the hospital and stood by Darlene's bed and wept. Her daughter-in-law never regained consciousness. Darlene died shortly after being taken in for surgery for a cerebral venous thrombosis. Adding to the tragedy, she was pregnant again. Shirley mourned with Darlene's family, but Jimmy Joe didn't attend the funeral. He couldn't face Darlene's parents, who were grief stricken. They later moved out of state and had little contact with their now orphaned grandson.

Jimmy Joe forbade anyone from telling Billy his mother was dead, or the circumstances. He and Shirley moved to be closer to the state prison, but didn't take the little boy to visit his father. Jimmy Joe visited several times a year but said James didn't deserve to have a relationship with his son. He said they would tell Billy everything someday, but they never did. Shirley was diagnosed with breast cancer when her grandson was sixteen and died last year, and Jimmy Joe had never explained the circumstances of his mother's disappearance to Billy."

I listened, feeling heartsick. There was too much ugliness in the world. I tried to imagine why Darlene would stay with a man who beat her—then I remembered my ex-boyfriend, Steve. He had an anger issue, and had frightened me several times, yelling at me. Then, shortly after one of those episodes, he proposed to me in a crowded restaurant in front of his parents and sister. When I said no and tried to walk away, he grabbed my arm around my wrist so hard, it left a mark for days and hurt. He had a problem with anger, too, and I'd stayed his girlfriend for several years. I told myself things would change, that we loved each other. I could understand why Darlene stayed.

I realized Mom was saying my name as I gripped my phone harder, trying to control my breathing. I reminded myself I was safe.

"Gracie? Are you alright?" Mom's voice was concerned. "I should have told you all this face to face. I'm sure it brings up bad memories of Steve."

"I'm okay, Mom. No worries," I said, hoping my voice wasn't shaky. "Yes, it brought up some memories, but I'm okay." Then I remembered the things Jimmy Joe and his grandson had done. "It doesn't excuse them from their behavior,"

"No, it doesn't," Mom agreed. "But it answers a few questions. Remember Roger pleading with the judge, saying that Jimmy wasn't an evil man? Anyway, Uncle Vern thought you should know."

We talked about other things for a few minutes before saying goodbye. Mom's voice was warm, and I tried to imagine growing up without her, much less not having a father around, either. Maybe I couldn't forgive Billy or his grandfather just yet, but it helped to know their story.

Seven

The Truck House
Marie

"Sometimes you just gotta look down the road and say, better times are coming."

~Grandma Edith

Frank parks our truck near his parents' truck house, outside the farmhouse. The little girls squeal because they want to go inside the truck house.

"Settle down," I say as Frank opens the door, and we get out.

Samuel is loading a few things into the cab.

He turns around, smiles, and says, "Who wants to take a tour of my truck house?"

The girls jump up and down. "Can we, Mama?" Julia asks and I nod.

Grandma Edith comes out the front door and hugs the little girls on their way to the truck. She pats her son on the shoulder and gives me a hug. "How are you holding up, dear? Lots of work to do, but we have better days ahead."

"Mama," calls Julia. "Come see me."

We walk over to the truck house, Edith leading the way. We climb the four steps and enter the little house in the kitchen area. Inside, the ceiling is almost seven feet tall, so the men can stand up and walk around. I glanced around and smile at the progress since our last visit. Edith and I had sewn simple flour sack curtains for the windows, but they hadn't been hung the last time I was here.

Frank pretends not to notice the girls tucked up into their bunk bed. He turns to me. "I thought the girls were in here, but I don't see them anywhere, do you, Mama?"

The giggling from the bunk bed at the other end of the house gets louder. I walk down the length of the truck house and admire the four long cushioned sleep benches that opened for storage, two on each side. I notice how Edith placed two trunks under the bunks at the other end. We can all sleep here tonight.

Frank and his father added four hinged, narrow tabletops on either side. He shows me how to raise them to eat, read, or write. Lower them to sleep. The tables weren't in place the last time I was here.

"Frank, this looks wonderful," I say. "You and your father can do just about anything you put your mind to do."

Edith shows me how she'd loaded dishes, cups, and silverware into the cupboards above the long counter. She'd torn old pillowcases into long strips and mounted them on top and bottom of the cupboards with thumb tacks to keep things from sliding around. The lids to the compartments kept them secured, and the strips of fabric kept the contents from breaking. She and Samuel are good partners in designing things, and my Frank can put their ideas into action.

"We'll make it work," I assure her.

We don't have a choice, do we? I think. Frank's family is my only family now. My folks and sister died 15 years ago, and this wonderful woman became my second mother, and was the only grandma my girls have ever known.

She nods and glances at the girls. "They think it's an adventure."

"Yes, they do. What's left to do in your house?" I ask.

"Not much. I thought we'd eat our last supper in there, wash up, and get the girls down to sleep in here. I have plenty of blankets and pillows up in the bunks, and did Frank show you how the windows open to let in a breeze? They have little cranks."

Frank and Samuel talk to the girls, showing them how to climb up and down, stepping up on the trunks and using the little rope and metal ladders.

I tell Frank, "We're fixing supper. Keep an eye on the girls, please."

As we walk toward the house, I hear the phone ring—three long and two short rings on the party line.

Edith hurries ahead of me. I hear her talking. "We're heading out in the morning. You're lucky you caught us, because they're turning off the phone tomorrow."

She listens then and is quiet. "Thank you, Mabel. Let me talk to everyone, and we'll call you back."

Edith turns to me. "That was my sister Mabel. She's worried about us. She's inviting us to come stay with them in Jubilee Junction, but I think Samuel has his mind made up. He wants to go West to find work and live in his truck house. What do you think?"

"I think Frank feels the same way, but it'd be challenging for two trucks to keep up with each other with all the stuff we've loaded up. It'll take more money for food and gas, and there's no guarantee of a job, is there? I guess we need to have that conversation with them," I reply.

We heat up the vegetable stew, add the biscuits baked yesterday, and pour the last milk into two cups for the girls and coffee for the rest of us. I'm on the verge of calling the family in, and then Edith and I burst into laughter. No chairs, no table. She'd sold or given away all her furniture.

I walk outside and tell Frank to put down the tables. Edith and I carry the food out to the truck with help from the men, who grabbed bowls and cups at the door and put them in place while we return to the kitchen for the last two bowls and cups of coffee. Edith tucked washcloths and spoons in her apron's pockets.

We sit at the improvised tables and eat our supper.

"We're camping, Mama," said Jessie looking around at us.

"I like the tables, Grandpa Samuel," Julia tells her grandpa.

The four of us adults glance at each other. Edith has a few tears in her eyes.

"Thank you, Julia. Your daddy figured out how to get them to lie down flat against the wall when we don't need them," Samuel explains. "He's a smart man, your daddy."

Frank grabs my free hand under the table as we eat every bite.

Afterward, we wash up the dishes in the house, dry them with flour sack towels, and pack the last of the kitchen stuff in the truck house.

The girls run around in the yard with their sweaters and coats on, while Edith relays the message from Mabel to the men.

Frank and Samuel exchange looks. Suddenly, Edith and I realize that there's more to this conversation than we realize.

Samuel clears his throat. "Edward and I've been talking. He feels real bad about us losing the farm. You know he tried to pay off that loan himself? He only raised $500, so he gave it up. But he has an idea. Why not leave the women folk and the girls with them in Jubilee Junction and park Frank's truck, while Frank and I go out West with the truck house?"

Edith considers it. "I suppose it makes sense. I'd sure miss you. The girls would miss their Papa. and so would Marie."

Samuel peers at her, and then at me. His eyes beg for our understanding. "I can't go to Jubilee Junction and just sit around. Frank and I plan to go West. If we don't find something, at least we aren't dragging you women and the girls along. There's plenty of room for Frank and me in the back of the truck house."

I turn away to hide my tears, and Frank comes over and traces the tears on my cheek with his thumb. "Listen, Marie. Pa's right. You and Mama and our girls would be safe at Aunt Mabel's. She's lonely now that her children are all grown up and out of the nest. She got that big house and just the two of them. We won't be gone that long."

I look at Edith and see the resignation in her eyes and sense the same weariness that threatens to engulf me. It would be simpler for the men to go and for us to stay behind. But I have never been without Frank in all the years since my parents and sister died.

I gaze up at Frank. "You and your father need to tell the girls."

He nods.

We call the girls, wash them up, get them in their nightgowns, and tuck them into their bunk beds, with several blankets to keep warm. At least they'll have tonight to sleep in their little bunk bed in Grandpa Samuel's camper.

Eight

Gracie Enlists David to Conduct Research
Gracie

"The problem with research, of course, is sometimes you don't know what you need to know."

~David

I drove home and researched flour sack dresses for an hour, starting with the links Charlotte sent me. I quickly became obsessed.

Starting in the 1800s, many products were shipped by barrel. As cotton became abundant and cheap, manufacturers switched over to cotton bags. During the late 1920s, women needed fabric to make a variety of things, ranging from dish towels to dresses to diapers. Manufacturers printed patterns and created instructions for how to use the bags to create other things.

One article on the flour sack towels website claimed it took three yards of fabric to make the average-sized dress. In 1927, it cost you sixty cents to order three yards of dress print cotton from the Sears and Roebuck catalog. However, it only took salvaging the Gingham Girl Flour sacks from two or three 100-pound bags of flour from the Plant Milling Company from St. Louis, Missouri, to do the same thing for free!

I sat back, amazed. *How many loaves of bread would one bag make? How much time would it take to go through that enormous bag of flour?* My head hurt trying to figure out the math, so I googled it. A two-pound loaf would need about 4 cups of flour (i.e., 2 pounds). So you'd get about 50 loaves from a hundred-pound sack.

As I kept reading, I learned thrifty housewives used the flour sack material to make diapers, dish towels, clothing, and curtains. One source estimated three and a half million women and children wore clothing made from flour sacks.

Then, during World War II, manufacturers switched to paper bags because we needed cotton for military uniforms.

A woman recounted, "My mom was born in 1939. Many of her clothes came from feed sacks when she was a child—a baby's gown could be made from a 5-pound sugar sack, a toddler was 2–3 sugar sacks, a small child was one 100-pound feed sack, an adult's dress was four 100-pound feed sacks, etc. Great-granny would pick the sacks, so they matched for whatever project we needed to complete."

"There was no better dish towel than a flour sack! The logos washed right off, and they turned white! I still have some. They were a wedding gift made by my husband's old auntie. She wouldn't give them to me until after the reception because she didn't think they were a *worthy* wedding gift! They're beautiful; they're embroidered on one corner."

I sat back, thinking about the research we'd done on World War II and World War I and the connections we'd made to our own family history. But I remembered little about the period between those wars. I'd never had to sew my own clothes or worry about finding fabric for kitchen towels, diapers, or curtains. I needed my historian husband's help to understand the Great Depression. As Aunt Violet might say, thank goodness I married a history teacher. I needed Aunt Violet, Aunt Maggie, and Uncle Vern to tell me anything they remembered from growing up during the depression.

After a hectic week of giving and grading finals and calculating final grades, David and I turned in grades online using the college portal—always a happy day. But this semester, instead of celebrating with a nice dinner out and maybe a movie, we picked up a pizza and turned our attention to the Crazy quilt and how pictures of it ended up in Katie's grandmother's photo album.

"David, I really need your help. I don't remember studying the 1930s," I confessed.

"History teacher at your service, ma'am." He held a slice of pizza up and nodded modestly.

As we chatted, I made a new *to-do* list. We had archives to check at *The Jubilee Times,* the library, and the museum. I asked David to go to the newspaper office and check there first thing tomorrow. Aunt Delores would show him around. I'd check at the library and then head to the museum.

We ate the pizza as we brainstormed ideas, and then snuggled and watched a movie.

Agatha walked around the house, sniffing us and the boxes we brought up from the basement.

"Think she smells my scented pinecones?" I asked.

"Could be. Hopefully, you don't have any catnip in these boxes." He grinned.

Agatha looked up at him just then and I wondered, *Does she know the word catnip?* Then I sighed. "David, I'm almost embarrassed to show you my holiday decorations. A snow globe or two, a couple of Christmas towels, pillows and candles—and yes, some scented pinecones."

David gazed at me, smiling. "Knowing your mother and my mother and our other extended family, what would happen if you put out the word that we lacked holiday decorations?"

I groan. "We would wake up and find a dozen boxes on the front porch by morning. Perhaps we can budget a little for decorations?"

David laughs. "Remember, my parents own a hardware store. I think we would get a hefty discount on anything we needed."

I nodded, grabbed my to-do clipboard, and wrote "Get decorations."

The next morning, we had a quick breakfast before I headed off to the library, and David drove to *The Jubilee Times* to use the archives upstairs.

Charlotte checked her online catalog of the Jubilee Junction Archives by the decade. "Let's start with the 1930s."

We went downstairs to Special Collections, which had file

cabinets, storage units, bookcases, a large table, and a few chairs. The archives held there focused on the history of Jubilee County and Jubilee Junction.

Charlotte and I examined materials in the filing cabinet and found a few interesting items, which we took to the table.

The first item was an essay by Cedar Falls native Ferner Nuhn, "Like a Thick Wall." Nuhn described being at a forced farm sale in 1933. Neighbors kept bids down low so the farmer could buy his things back, for pennies on the dollar. Married to the prolific writer Ruth Suckow, Ferner Nuhn worked as a writer in the Department of Agriculture under Henry Wallace, a fellow Iowan. The essay appeared in the *Nation* magazine and was later posted on the website www.historymatters.edu.

"Like a Thick Wall: Blocking Farm Auctions in Iowa"

"*Nation* magazine reporter Ferner Nuhn witnessed such an auction sale in Iowa and described this practice in March 1933. These efforts saved the livelihood of many South Dakota and Iowa farmers who were devastated by the Depression, but they were not enough. Between 1930 and 1935 about 750,000 farms were lost through foreclosure and bankruptcy sales."

His description of the farm sale brought tears to my eyes: "The silence of the farmers is like a thick wall. The rigmarole of the auctioneer beats against it, and falls back in his face. The farmer holding the mare stands with his head hanging. At last, without raising his eyes, he says, "Fifteen dollars." This is a new and distressing business to him, and he is ashamed to make a bid of less than that...."

We briefly checked other exhibit items from the 1930s but found nothing else that seemed relevant, so we returned those materials to the filing cabinets. Then we went upstairs. Charlotte focused on her work, while I made copies of and emailed the essay to myself and David. Although disappointed, I was determined to keep looking.

As I was finishing up, I got a call from David, sounding excited. "Guess what, Gracie? I found several articles to show you. I've made copies. Are you at the museum or library? I'll come to you."

When he arrived, he had a folder of half a dozen items. Charlotte and I sat down to look at what he'd found.

The Jubilee Times, March 6, 1933.

In response to a month-long run on the banks, President FDR declared a local Bank holiday, March 6 to March 9, 1933, shutting down the banking system. Congress passed the Emergency Banking Act, creating a guaranteed 100 percent deposit insurance in the reopened banks. People rushed to the banks, withdrawing all their money. Within a week of the Banking Act, people were standing in line to deposit their money.

The Jubilee Times, May 14, 1933. *Bank Manager Shot & Killed at Prairie Falls Bank.*

Howard Moser shot Thomas Jenkins, the Prairie Falls branch bank manager. This incident happened on Friday, May 14, after the bank foreclosed on Moser's farm because he had defaulted. According to Bank President Edward Richardson, the bank manager died of his injuries on the scene. The Jubilee County Sheriff arrested the farmer after the incident, which took place mid-day. Several witnesses identified the shooter.

The Jubilee Times and The Des Moines Register, spring and summer 1933. David found half a dozen articles about nearly three hundred banks failing in Iowa and surrounding states.

One article estimated that 1 in 10 farms changed hands during the Depression, with many families leaving the Midwest because of the dust bowl.

At the bottom of the stack, I discovered articles about farm sales and foreclosures forcing farm families to leave rural Iowa and look for jobs out West.

We sat down at a worktable where David had spread out the clippings. He wore a serious expression. "I think we need to consider the historical and social context for this story. The Great Depression lasted about ten years and did tremendous damage to our nation and our state. Bank failures, foreclosures, and losing family farms—these are destabilizing experiences, traumatic, and stressful. You can see why people might not want to remember them. Many farm families moved west, others moved to town, and within the space of a generation or two, their lives were totally upended."

David exhaled. "For example, my mother's grandfather left to live with an aunt and uncle in Wisconsin when he was only 14. His family lost their farm and couldn't stay together because they couldn't feed their eight children. They split up the oldest six children and sent them to various relatives. People might not want to remember that sort of thing. So whatever information we find, we need to remember that these were some of the toughest times ever for farmers and families in the Midwest."

Charlotte and I glanced at each other across the table, and she nodded. I wondered, not for the first time, about her family stories, and when I'd learn more about my friend who was born to a white father and a Meskwaki mother. I showed David the essay we'd found by Ferner Nuhn, and he read it with interest, making a copy for himself.

After another half hour of looking through the articles, I gathered things up into a folder and packed my iPad in my messenger bag. I thanked Charlotte for her help and promised to follow up once I showed the images of the women to my family.

David and I walked out into the crisp December air to our cars, and I followed him home, thinking about what it must have been like to experience the Great Depression. David's speech at the library sobered me. I realized we had a more complex puzzle than I'd anticipated. David's point was valid. People didn't like to remember things that were painful, especially when it happened when they were children.

I shivered, getting out of the car. The wind was blowing, but I wondered what had happened to Jessie and Julia when they were children, and their parents and grandparents had lost the farm? What might we discover, and how was I going to fulfill my promise?

Nine

Sleepover in the Truck House
Marie

"It's going to be alright. Have faith. Things are going to get better."

~Grandma Edith

*G*randpa Samuel read them a story and said a prayer. He and Edith gave them both a hug and a kiss, and so did Frank. The three of them stepped away so that I could adjust the pillows and kiss both girls.

Edith points up at the ceiling, and I notice Samuel and Frank have installed a little curtain so we can give the girls some privacy. I adjust the curtains and say, "Goodnight girls."

A little voice said, "Mama, I love my new bed." It was Jessie.

"I'm glad, honey," I reply.

Julia adds, "It's very comfortable, Mama. Don't be sad we lost our house."

I am thankful it's too dark for them to see my face. "Alright," I answer. "I won't be sad," as tears roll off my cheeks.

The men step outside to take a last walk around the property.

Edith regards me with compassion. "They're such sweet little things. And too smart."

She points out that the benches closest to the girl's bunks are for me and Frank. About three feet wide, and almost six feet long, they have sleeping bags on them, covered with several blankets and a pillow. The benches weren't finished on my last visit. Edith and Samuel are sleeping on the benches closest to the side door.

"I'm alright. Thanks." I fight the urge to drop to the bench, weariness almost overtaking me.

Instead, I go inside the house to use the bathroom. I know I'll have to use the chamber pot in the truck house, but it's a good reason to step outside.

Frank and his father are sitting on the porch steps, chatting. I overhear one of them mention Route 66 as I walk by. Frank reaches for my hand when I walk back from the bathroom. I sit down and listen as they debate where to go to search for work.

"I hear fruit farmers out in California need help," Frank leans forward. "Someone told me that at the farm sale. But isn't everyone going to head there?"

His father nods. "Edward wants to talk to us. There's going to be some government program out West, and he thinks we would be good candidates for supervisors."

Frank squeezes my hand. "You're tired, honey. We'll be in shortly. Go get comfy on that bench bed and see what you think."

I say goodnight and walk to the truck. It's quiet. Edith sits on her bed, brushing her hair. I walk past her, and she tells me, "It's going to be alright. Have faith. Things are going to get better."

I nod, hoping her faith would be enough for both of us.

The girls are asleep because I can hear their soft breathing. I pulled back the thin curtain and realize it's an old bed sheet. That clever mother-in-law of mine. Then I saw there was another sheet between the front set of benches and ours.

I take off my shoes, lie down, and find it more comfortable than I'd imagined. There was a gap between my bed and Frank's, so we'd be close, but we wouldn't be in the same bed. I'd taken off the apron but kept on my sweater and coat for warmth. I pull up the blankets.

A few minutes later, Frank comes in and closes the sheet curtain behind him. He removes his shoes and crawls into bed. He put out his arm, and I did the same, and we held onto each other's hands. Then, he whispers, "I'm coming over."

We squeeze onto my bench and cuddle with his arms around me. He whispers, "I wondered if we could both fit." I try not to giggle, but I can hardly breathe, squeezed between the truck's wall and Frank's chest. But it's comforting to have his embrace. How will I sleep alone when he and Samuel leave?

"I'm going to miss you something fierce," he whispers. Then he kisses me and goes back over to his bench.

The cushioned bench feels good on my weary body. I roll over, gather up the blankets, hear the soft murmurs of Samuel and Edith—and then nothing.

In the morning, we get up early. I tell the girls we'll eat breakfast when we arrive in Jubilee Junction.

Frank picks up little Jessie and we head for our truck. It's chilly, so we let the girls take a blanket with them.

His folks get into the cab of the big truck house, and we follow them to the county road. We don't look back. There isn't much to see but empty buildings and broken promises.

On the drive, Frank points out several surrounding farms already foreclosed on and shakes his head. "All this good Iowa farmland gone to waste. Who's going to buy this land? Who's going to grow the crops to feed the country?"

I fight tears as I stare outside at the familiar rolling hills. Too many of my friends have lost their farms, too. I feel like one of my strawberry plants ripped up by its roots. I miss my home and my familiar dirt.

The girls snuggle up in the middle, keeping warm. They chatter to each other about sleeping in the truck house. It's an adventure for them.

We arrive in Jubilee Junction half an hour later, pulling up in front of the large Queen Anne house where my aunt and uncle live.

They walk out the front door to greet us, but I notice Uncle Edward looks tired. There's a weariness in his eyes that I don't recall. Aunt Mabel hugs us all and tells the girls how happy she is that we came to visit.

Jessie hugs her back and says, "Well, we can't stay, Aunt Mabel, 'cause our Daddy's taking us to California. We're camping out in the truck."

My mother-in-law and I stare at the men.

Grandpa Samuel says. "Girls, let's go inside Aunt Mabel's house. Your Daddy and I need to talk to you about something."

We walk up the steps and into the front parlor and sit down on one of the two large horsehair couches, and Mabel and Edward join us. Frank put his arms out to the girls, and they climbed up on his lap. "We think you girls, Grandma, and Mama should stay here with Aunt Mabel and Uncle Edward while Grandpa Samuel and I drive out West to find work. It'll be hard work to drive two trucks, and I'm not too sure about the tires on my truck."

"We want to go with you, Daddy," wails Jessie. "We want to sleep in our bunk." Her older sister, Julia, listens quietly, rubbing her little sister's back.

"I know, Jessie girl. But we think this is the best plan, and I need you girls to help me out here. I'm gonna miss you both something fierce. I need you to take care of your mama and grandma." Frank hugs the girls.

He gives Jessie time to get it all out, and Julia climbs off his lap, comes over to me, and hugs me. "We'll be together, Mama, right? We'll take care of each other."

I hold my eldest. She has been my sweetness for the past eight years.

"Yes, Julia. The girls stay together," I assure her.

Jessie got up and came over to me, and the three of us hug and cry.

Aunt Mabel says, "We have plenty of room for you here. Should we go upstairs and look around?"

We all stand up then, and Grandma Edith takes Julia's hand, as I take Jessie's. The men watch as we walk to the stairs.

Samuel checks his watch. "We'll start unloading Frank's truck."

Ten

Settling in at Aunt Mabel's
Marie

"In the Great Depression in which I grew up and remember vividly, unemployment was over 25 percent, and over 35 percent where I lived. A grown man would work all day, 16 hours, for a dollar. I remember hundreds of people walking by, people who had come down from the North just to get warm. They would come to our house as beggars even though they might have a college education. People didn't have money. They bartered; they'd trade eggs or pigs. It was just completely different."
~Jimmy Carter

We explore the upstairs, while the three men unpack Frank's truck, putting things in the basement and parking Frank's truck in the shed by the side of the house.

As we walk upstairs, we discover four bedrooms, several closets in the hallway, and a nice modern bathroom.

Mabel led us to the first bedroom and told me it would be my room. I've never slept in such a lovely room with creamy beige wallpaper with pink cabbage roses. There's a full size bed with a large headboard, a long dresser with a mirror, and closet in the corner. Two large windows give us a view of the garden in the backyard.

Bless their hearts, the men carry my furniture up to our bedroom.

I drop the leaves on grandma's table and put two chairs in our room and leave the other two in the hallway to go into the girls' room. The men carry the chest of drawers into our room, along with the bookcase. I'll fill the shelves and drawers later. I lay one of my treasured quilts from my grandma on the foot of the bed.

Aunt Mabel wanders over to look. "Lovely. You quilt, dear?"

"Yes, when I have time. My grandma taught me."

"Gorgeous. Look at those tight little stitches. Fine craftsmanship. I can't wait to introduce you and Edith to my quilting circle."

We take the girls next door and show them a beautiful bedroom with two twin beds. The walls are covered in more of the cabbage rose wallpaper. Mabel's girls grew up in this room. Now they're both grown and out in the world. The beds had fluffy pink bedspreads with a quilt underneath, nice beige rugs, and pink and white curtains. The girls gaze around the room in delight.

"Look Mama," Jessie squeals. "There's a little room here." She opens the door of the walk-in closet. "This could be our playhouse."

Frank carries in their battered suitcase and the small box of toys and books. I put their clothes away in the dresser, one drawer each for underwear, socks and pjs. Three little worn flour sack dresses each in the closet. They were wearing their sweaters and jackets.

Aunt Mabel watches with troubled eyes. We didn't have much in terms of clothing or toys for the girls.

Samuel and Edith were across the hall. It was a roomy house with one more bedroom down the hall for Edward and Mabel, and a door leading up to the attic.

We walk downstairs for breakfast. Oatmeal on the stove, with real cream, sugar, coffee, milk, thick slices of bread and butter and strawberry jam on the table. I watched my girls tuck into their breakfast, looking at the abundance of food with appreciative eyes. They were good girls with polite table manners.

The men were talking quietly at the table, drinking coffee. Samuel and Frank wouldn't leave right away. We'd all worked hard over the past two weeks and were exhausted.

Uncle Edward has a small tablet of paper and a pencil next to his plate and scribbles things from time to time.

Frank says, "Uncle Edward, we counted two farm sales advertised on the way down here. It's going to be a ghost town up there. Who's going to buy those farms? How are we going to feed the country if we don't have people working on that farmland?"

Samuel nods. "Yes, I noticed those sales as well. Did you notice the Browns packing up across the way?"

Uncle Edward agrees. "It's a terrible time for our state and our country. I've been a banker for almost forty years, and I've seen nothing like this before. It's heartbreaking."

He takes a sip of his coffee and then stares at his nephew and brother-in-law. "I contacted my friend in the congressman's office, and I want to talk to you about a good opportunity when I get home tonight. There are plans for conservation projects out West, planting trees, building dams and shelters, and you two have the skills to be supervisors. My friend's checking on a few details and sending me a wire this afternoon."

Samuel and Frank are eating oatmeal, too, and nod in agreement.

I watch the girls eating, and eat my oatmeal, savoring the lovely taste of fresh cream and brown sugar.

I watch the men, dreading the idea of being separated from Frank. He's been my rock since I was 18 years old. We got married at the Jubilee County Courthouse the same week that we put my poor parents and sister in the ground. The pandemic left me an orphan, but my parents loved Frank, were friends and neighbors with his folks, and knew we were getting married. That gave me some comfort. We hadn't spent a night apart since then. And now, I feared that he'd go out West never to be seen again.

The girls finish every bite of their breakfast and thank Aunt Mabel. They drink every drop of milk. Julia carries her bowl to the counter and comes back for Jessie's. She tells her sister, "You carry the spoons."

Then Julia returns for the two little glasses.

Aunt Mabel observes, "Well, I'm going to enjoy having you girls here. Maybe you can help me train Uncle Edward to take his dishes over to the sink," as she cast a sideways look at her husband, while the little girls giggle.

Uncle Edward takes his coffee cup over to the sink, grins, and says, "Well, I'd like to peek inside of that truck house. I need to leave for the bank in an hour. Let's take a quick look, shall we girls?"

The men get up, and the girls follow.

I help Edith and Aunt Mabel straighten up the kitchen.

Edith remarks, "I told you that those girls are little angels."

We troop out for a tour of the truck house.

The mail man walks by. A neighbor walks his dog. Another neighbor sweeps her front porch steps, and her husband reads the newspaper on the swing. Several other neighbors are standing outside, watching us from across the street.

Edward looks around at his neighbors and waves. "Shall we let everyone get a tour?" He gestures. "C'mon over, folks."

We watch as Edward escorts his neighbors in by two or three. Frank and Samuel explain the features, while the little girls giggle and climb into their bunk beds, declaring how comfy they are.

My mother-in-law put an arm around my shoulders.

"We got us some clever men, don't we, Marie?"

People shake their heads in amazement as they exit the truck house door.

"I'd like to take a trip in that truck," the neighbor's husband announces.

"It's very comfy," the dog walker agrees.

"I like those benches and tables. What a clever idea!"

"My children would love those bunks."

We love hearing our men praised.

Finally, Edward waves and walks off to the bank.

The girls chatter, excited to be in the truck house.

However, it's time for the men to lighten the load. After all, they don't need all the bedding, dishes, and other things.

Mabel found three empty cardboard boxes, and we got to work. She asks me to carry a box of bedding up to the attic with her. We take a pencil and write my name on the box. Then, as we turn to go back downstairs, I notice a sewing room on a lower level of the attic. It's fixed up real nice, with a treadle sewing machine, bench, and four shelves full of fabric. There are several large windows and a built-in counter below the shelves.

Aunt Mabel turns to me. "When I was younger and had little ones, I made all their dresses. I have arthritis now, so I don't sew as much. But I wonder if you could find something to do with all this fabric?"

I can't speak. I run my hands over the fabric, enjoying the sensation, looking at the colors and patterns, already thinking of what I might make for my little girls. I nod, staring at the treadle sewing machine, fighting tears. "Yes, thank you."

The sewing machine was in lovely shape, a Singer Model 66. Mama's machine had given out last year, and even Frank couldn't fix it. I want to sit down on that little bench and get to rocking that treadle!

"I got some dresses in my back closet that I think would fit you, from what my girls left behind. They aren't fancy, but I think you'd like them, and I got a few things for my sister, too. I know you've all been through hard times. I bet I can find you some patterns here for your girls. *The Jubilee Times* has been printing them."

I follow her to the closet at the end of the hallway downstairs. Aunt Mabel opens the door and takes out half a dozen dresses and put them in my arms. "Go try these things on, Marie. You can have all of them. The girls left them here, and I never got around to doing anything with them. There are also a few sweaters in here, an old coat, and who knows what else? Try those on, and if they fit, you can have them. I suppose you can always take them apart and sew something else with the fabric."

I took the armful of dresses down to our bedroom and slipped out of the worn house dress and apron I was wearing. Both were made from flour sacks but faded after being washed on an old washboard. When our wringer washing machine broke last year, Frank couldn't find the parts to repair it. I put on the first dress, a cheery floral on a blue background, and the door opened. It was Frank.

"Aunt Mabel said you needed me?" He smiles, seeing me partly undressed.

"Can you zip me up?" I ask, my voice shaky with emotion.

He does and kisses my neck. "You look beautiful," he says.

I stare at the collection of dresses on the bed and feel overwhelmed.

A yellow dress with a gathered waist, a floral housedress, and a red dress with a gathered waist and high collar. The floral dress fits well, and I caress the silky fabric of the skirt. A pink dress with little bows on the sleeves peeks out from under the pile of dresses.

I throw my arms around Frank and sob as he holds me tight.

"There, there. It's going to be alright, Marie. Don't know if I'll ever understand you women. Someone gives you pretty clothes and you cry. You won't catch me crying over a new pair of overalls." He holds me tighter. "I'm going to miss you something fierce."

Eleven

Christmas Trees and Cats
Gracie

"Cats and Christmas trees should be kept apart. Anyone who's seen National Lampoon's Christmas Vacation knows that."

~David

A few days later, I was busy decorating and wrapping a few presents while David was out of the house. Usually, Agatha would be right there with me when I wrapped gifts. She loved the crinkle of wrapping paper and tried to help with the tissue paper, but not today.

David, his father, and his younger brother Alex were outside, putting up lights on the patio and roof. I decided no good could come of me standing outside in the cold, worrying about them being up on ladders hanging lights. So I listened to Christmas music as I examined our four new boxes of decorations.

Agatha perched on her cat tree, looking suspicious.

David and I had wrestled a lovely young pine tree into the house, gotten it into the corner tree stand, covered the base in foil, and sprinkled orange rinds underneath.

We'd read the article about trees and cats again. I filled a small spray bottle with apple cider vinegar, but after spraying the lower branches, I backed off and exhaled. I didn't like the smell. Hopefully, Agatha wouldn't either.

I focused on the top half of the tree with the decorations, making sure that I put little bits of tin foil here and there as a deterrent.

I found an old baby gate in a corner of the basement storeroom and leaned it up against my tub, filled with a few gifts. While I hadn't figured out what to do with the baby gate, someone posted a picture of their tree with a baby gate in front. It served as another barrier to the cat getting at the tree. I thought the tree would fit the space in the corner, but the tree was bigger.

Someone knocked at the door, and I let Mom in, warning her about the smell. I was still holding the spray bottle. She sniffed.

"That looks festive." She examined the Christmas tree, and noted Agatha retreating into one of her little boxes on the cat tree.

I showed Mom how I planned to use the tub for our gifts. "That way, nothing important gets ruined."

"Can you put the bottle down?" Mom backed away. "I keep waiting for you to spray me, if I get out of line."

So I put it down.

"I wanted to check on how you're doing with your research," Mom admitted.

"We've hit some brick walls. We need more names and information to get anywhere with the genealogy websites. Doesn't it seem strange that Katie's mother didn't talk about her own mother and grandmother more, and the Great Depression? I thought that generation was full of stories."

Mom agreed. "Do you have time to run over to the farmhouse? I have Aunt Violet in the car, and I'd like to show her the album, if you still have it."

I glanced over at my messenger bag. "Yes, I'd like that, mom. Charlotte and I found a set of photos of a quilt auction in the library's special collections. I wanted to ask Aunt Violet in case she recognized any of the women."

"Stay away from the Christmas tree, cat." I grabbed my coat, messenger bag, and purse, and followed Mom to the car.

David and his brother were busy stringing lights up on the farmhouse, while their father, Harry, supervised from the ground. They waved hello at my mother and Aunt Violet.

I told Harry where we were going, and he responded, "OK, Gracie. Just wait until you get back! It's going to look very festive."

I stared at the half dozen tubs already unloaded and wondered what else he had in the back of his pickup truck. What were those tall and wide shapes covered up by the canvas tarps? It was safe to leave these guys, right?

Twelve

Charting a Path West
Marie

*"The CCC planted more than three billion trees and con-
structed trails and shelters in more than 800 parks nationwide
during its nine years of existence. The CCC helped to shape the
modern national and state park systems we enjoy today."*
~The Civilian Conservation Corps

After supper, we clear the table and do the
dishes. I glance around my aunt's roomy kitchen, still amazed by
the large counters, cupboards, running water, gas stove, and an
electric icebox! It is a marked contrast to the cramped quarters
I'd called a kitchen. I hadn't been here in almost two years as our
chores kept us quite busy on the farm.

Mabel and Edith finish drying the dishes while I wipe down
the countertops, glancing over at Frank. He sits with his father
and uncle at the dining room table, drinking coffee and talking.
Edward has a tablet of paper, a pen, and a large yellow envelope
in front of him.

Frank signals me to join him, as Aunt Mabel says, "Who wants
a cookie? I think I saw some around here." Jessie and Julia giggle as
she opens her large pantry closet. Edith joins her and they emerge
with a cookie jar.

I put the wash rag on the sink, take off my apron, put it over
a chair, and reach up to smooth my hair before walking in and
sitting down by Frank.

Uncle Edward refers to his notes on the tablet. "My cousin sent the information. He works for our Iowa congressman. There's a new program called the CCC, the Civilian Conservation Corps. It's going to put thousands of unemployed young men, ages 18–25, to work doing lots of different jobs across the country. They need experienced supervisors to help plant trees, clear brush, and build various buildings. And you two are more than qualified for the job. After all, you've built that fine camper out there. I've seen Frank work with metal, and I've seen you building things, Samuel. You've been a carpenter and inventor as long as you've been farming. They would be lucky to have you."

Uncle Edward leans back and clears his throat. "It turns out there's a CCC camp that's going to start up in Wyoming. You'll be just two states away from your girls, and the Army is running it, so I mentioned Edward was a World War One veteran. You're to report to Camp Fremont, on the south shores of Fremont Lake next week. It'll take you four or five days to drive there on Highway 20. But this way, you won't be so far away from your girls. There's a lot to get done before the first batch of young men arrive in a few weeks. You can do some good and teach some young men how to work with wood and metal, plant trees, and build."

He hands Samuel a big yellow envelope and a smaller one. "Here's the letter to give to the camp commander, and here's a little something to help you on the way." His voice is gruff. "I'm sorry we couldn't save your farm."

Samuel takes the envelope. "Thank you, Edward." His voice is thick with emotion.

There's cash in the smaller envelope.

The two men look at each other for a moment. Then, without a word, they get up and walk to the basement.

Frank glances at me. I can't speak. Wyoming, not California. I exhale. That's a lot closer, fewer mountains to cross, maybe safer.

I gesture to the basement door.

Frank grins. "I think they're celebrating with a drink of whiskey. Prohibition may be over, but Aunt Mabel says she won't have it upstairs, so they go down to the basement. Uncle Edward has two chairs down there by a little table, and sometimes he sits down there to think."

"Did you see the money?" I ask.

"Yes," Frank nods. "Uncle Edward gave us $50 for gas and another $25 for food. My father has a little money set aside, so we should be all right."

He takes my hand as the girls come in, bringing us a cookie. "Well, thank you, girls."

Mabel looks at the open basement door. But she and her sister have smiles on their faces that tell me they know the news.

Edith smiles. "You see, Marie. It's going to work out, just like I told you. The good Lord is in control and better days are coming."

Mabel looks at the girls. "Why don't you folks go up and give the girls a good wash up and tuck them in? They're looking tired."

We take the girls upstairs for a nice bath and tuck them into their beds in their new bedroom. Their little nightgowns are getting too small and faded from being washed, but they don't seem to mind at all. I'd have to fix that.

Jessie asks, "Daddy, will you be here in the morning?"

Frank assures her he will be here. "We're leaving in a few days," he says.

She rolls over on her tummy, and Frank sits down beside her and rubs her back. Jessie's sweet little face relaxes, and I smile at her daddy.

I sit on Julia's bed and listen to her telling me all her favorite things about the room. "...and I like the closet and the bookcase and the pretty curtains and bedspreads. We're lucky, aren't we, Mama? Those girls grew up, so we get their room now."

I nod. "Yes, Julia, I think you're right. We're lucky, or your grandma would say we're blessed."

After we get the girls settled, I use the bathtub and think I've died and gone to heaven. There's a fancy bottle of bubbles, and I add just a capful, like Aunt Mabel says, and it makes a tub full of pinkish suds. I sink down, soak, and marvel at how relaxing it is. Best of all, I don't have to worry about people banging on the door, because my aunt's house has a bathroom on each floor. Afterwards, I wrap myself up in a towel, put on my shabby old robe, and scoot across the hall to our bedroom.

Frank sits on the bed, looking around.

"Your turn," I tell him. Frank takes a bundle of clothes and leaves the room.

I towel myself off and my hair, too, thinking I hadn't felt this clean for a very long time. I put on my nightgown and walk around the room, marveling at the contrast between my shabby old home and this nicely furnished room.

A few minutes pass, Frank comes in wearing a pair of pajama pants and an undershirt and carrying his dirty clothes. He looks refreshed, with his hair wet, and smiling. I point to the little pile of dirty clothing in the corner, thinking I'll tackle that problem tomorrow.

We turn down the bed, crawl in, and talk about all that had to be done before he leave. Frank turns out the lamp on the table next to him, and puts his arms around me, drawing me to his chest. He kissed me gently. A few minutes later, I hear his soft snores and try to relax. For now, we are all together. I want to memorize his shape and smell, the bristles of his beard on my shoulder, and the touch of his lips on mine.

How will I get through six months or a year apart? I don't know. As I drift off to sleep, a few tears trickle down my cheeks. I think of my parents, and one scripture my preacher father loved to quote comes to mind. Proverbs 3:5, *Trust in the Lord with all thine heart; and lean not unto thine own understanding.*

I repeat it several times before I finally fall asleep.

Thirteen

Apple Cider Vinegar & Aunt Violet's Memories
Gracie

"Write it down, Gracie. We made two Crazy quilts in 1933."
~Aunt Violet

*O*nce I was settled in the car, Aunt Violet called hello from the front seat, and then sniffed, "Gracie, honey, have you been cleaning with apple cider vinegar? I use white vinegar myself."

I described the article that David had found about *cat-proofing* a Christmas tree. Then I sniffed. Aunt Violet was right. My holiday sweatshirt smelled of vinegar.

Mom made a funny noise that ended in a cough.

We arrived at Mark and Kathy's farmhouse and got out of the car. Mom sent a text, and Kathy opened the door. "The twins are napping. Thanks for not ringing the doorbell."

We walked in and sat down at the dining room table, where Katie was waiting. I sat down, got out the photo album, still wrapped up in the tea towel, and handed my Aunt Violet a pair of cotton gloves. Her eyes were sparkling with adventure.

"Please look through the pictures and tell me if you recognize anything or anyone," I said, sounding more formal than I'd intended. I dug in the messenger bag for my notebook and two pens.

She examined each page of the album, sometimes flipping back to the previous page. Aunt Violet looked up. "Oh my, I hadn't thought about these days in forever and ever. Is this one of Mama's old albums? I don't remember this one."

"No, it's from Kathy's Mom—Katie. It belonged to her grandmother," I explained.

"Well, that's the Jubilee quilting club, and my mother's friend, what was her name? M— something. Marge? No, Mabel. Married to a banker, and they lived in that lovely Queen Anne over on Second street. What was his name? Notice that older woman and that younger one? I recollect they came to Jubilee to stay with Mabel after they lost their farm. They had a truck house." She turned the page. "That's the truck—right there."

Katie interrupted. "That's my Grandma Marie, and Great-Grandma Edith, Violet."

"Oh, my goodness. Marie and Edith, of course. See that little girl with her back to the camera? That's your Grandma Grace as a girl, and I'm back here in the corner. She was eleven and I would have been nine, but we always tagged along to the Jubilee quilt club with Mama and Grandma. Those two little girls are Jessie and Julia, and one of them is your mama?"

I glanced at Katie, who was hanging onto every word. She murmured, "Yes. That's really my mother and Aunt Julia as children?" Kathy sat beside her mother, and the two grandfathers sat on the other side of the table, drinking coffee. Aunt Violet continued turning the pages, murmuring to herself.

I sighed, got out my phone, and called David. "How's that exterior illumination going? I'm over at Kathy and Mark's, and Aunt Violet just cracked the case wide open. You need to hear this, and I think we should record it, if that's alright," I said, grabbing my iPad out of the messenger bag.

"We're about halfway done with the roof, Gracie. The forecast for tomorrow is rain and wind. Can we possibly hold off, so we can get it done during the daylight?" David asked.

I put it on speakerphone and looked around. Katie nodded, and so did Aunt Violet and Mom, but they were clearly disappointed.

"OK, David. Finish up and we'll figure out when to meet again."

I overheard Aunt Violet saying something. "Aunt Violet, hush up, and let me do a quick video," I fiddled with the camera on the iPad.

"Write it down, Gracie. We made two Crazy quilts in 1933," Aunt Violet stated.

I stared at her. "Charlotte and I noticed a photo with two Crazy quilts. I thought I was mistaken."

Aunt Violet looked at me prim and proper. "I guess we'll talk about that later, when it's more convenient."

Mom raised her eyebrows at me, and I knew I was in trouble with Aunt Violet. I couldn't remember her being snarky with me before, and we needed her help. However, I also knew that Aunt Violet would forgive all.

OK, I needed to write it down. I turned off the camera and found the note app. I created a new note: *The Jubilee quilting club made two Crazy quilts in 1933. Ask Aunt Violet for more information. Apologize to Aunt Violet!* I put the iPad down.

I looked up, and everyone had scattered. Only Mom, Katie, and Aunt Violet were still sitting at the dining room table.

Katie reached over and touched Aunt Violet's arm. "Thank you! I can't wait to hear the entire story later." She glanced at Mom and stood up. "I have laundry to fold, of course."

"Need help? I've got a few minutes." Mom stood up.

Aunt Violet, still absorbed by the photo album, flipped back and forth.

I scooted over and took one of her hands. "I'm sorry. I was rude."

She looked up, and I knew she'd forgive me.

"We could always label the pictures on the back," I offered. "I have sticky notes in my bag."

She brightened up, and we got busy making notes of people's names and relationships in my notebook. An hour slipped by, and it was time to pack up and take her home for supper. We'd made progress on at least half the photos.

She gave me a long hug and whispered, "If that husband of yours wasn't so handsome, I might have fussed longer. I guess I can wait to tell the story."

Fourteen

Shopping for the Men
Marie

"I'm gonna miss you something fierce."

~Frank Olson

*E*dith and I are going town today to buy clothing for the men for their new jobs. We pick out three work shirts each, pants, union suits, socks, and work boots. Their patched coveralls and faded work shirts need to be replaced. Uncle Edward had handed us some money this morning and said to go shopping for the men. We thanked him. We had both saved up a little egg money and wanted to be sure that they were ready for their trip.

As we head towards the cash register, I notice a display of zippered sweatshirts, and we add two of those to our load along with a package of handkerchiefs.

As we pass by the shoe department, Edith pause. "We should get a pair of shoes for ourselves," she says. "When we bring the girls, we'll be too busy getting them fixed up."

We try on several pairs and do quick calculations. We have enough money to get a nicer pair for church and a pair for everyday use. I glance down at my broken-down shoes and then over at Edith's. They are held together with metal hog rings. We'd both gone without to keep the children in decent shoes.

When we get back from shopping, there is a line of people going into the truck house for a look, including young James O'Connor, the editor of *The Jubilee Times*. He has his Kodak Brownie camera and is admiring the exterior of the truck house.

"This is amazing," he says. "Can you imagine taking a trip in this rig?"

Edith nods. "Don't have to imagin," she quips. "Actually, I have. It wasn't this fancy, but we took it out to California a few years ago."

James takes pictures inside for the weekly newspaper and interviews Frank and Samuel about building it.

Julia and Jessie show him how to get in and out of the bunk beds. Edith watches and smiles.

Aunt Mabel, standing by the door of the truck, waves at her sister. "Just think, if we charged a nickel admission, we'd be rich!"

"Those girls aren't shy," Edith observes proudly.

We go into the house, put on our new everyday shoes, and put our nice shoes away in the closet. We put the men's clothing away upstairs, get lunch on the table, and coax the girls into eating and playing inside.

The men finish eating and focused on checking over the truck house for the trip. They've already changed the oil, checked the tires, and inspected the spare tire.

They'd found a road map at a nearby Amoco station and spread it out on the dining room table to plan their route.

Julia looks over her daddy's shoulder at the map on the table. "Iowa, Nebraska, and Wyoming. U.S. 20 all the way!" she read out loud.

"Good job. That's right, Miss Julia," her Daddy says. His finger points to Camp Fremont near a lake. "That's where we're headed."

Frank gives me the truck keys. I had driven it on our back roads between our place, the country school, and the farm, but can't imagine driving it around Jubilee Junction. He holds my hand for a moment after putting the keys in my palm.

He smiles. "Keep these safe for me, alright, Marie?"

I drop them into my apron's pocket.

We walk to the store with the girls and get them shoes that afternoon. Jessie and Julia loved trying on shoes, and we find some little lace-up everyday shoes and another pair of Mary Janes for church. We have enough money left over for two packages of socks and two sticks of candy for each girl.

With shopping done, Edith and I spend the rest of the afternoon packing the men's clothing in the benches of the truck house and getting the interior ready for them. The girls play up in their bunk while the three of us women work.

Edith and Mabel make a special supper that night, and we try to be festive. But there is a pervasive sadness underneath it all. We don't know how long the two men will be gone.

Samuel says, "We checked into the CCC at the Jubilee Junction library because your neighbor mentioned they had fliers there. These young men sign up for a six-month stretch. They earn room and board plus $25.00 a month, and $20.00 gets sent home to their families. We haven't been told our wages, but you'll get some of the money to help you here."

Edward replies, "We're family, Samuel. Your girls are welcome here. I don't think they're going to need much money. Don't you worry."

Frank agrees and says, "We could be gone for six months, or longer, and they could move us around to different camps as the need arises." He glances at his little girls, who are eating their chocolate pudding for dessert and already looking sleepy from the busy day. Julia chats with her sister about shoe shopping, and I'm not sure that they understood what he is saying.

We give the girls a quick wash up and get them into their night-gowns. Frank and I crowd onto Julia's bed with Jessie tucked under my arms and read two stories with them before tucking them in. Frank hugged them extra-long, and little Jessie clings to him while I sit on Julia's bed and hold her close.

I whisper, "We're going to be alright."

Finally, we stand. I think, *children remember nights like this forever.* I fumble for my hankie.

"Good night, Miss Julia and Jessie Girl," Frank tells the girls.

When we finally climb into bed, I cling to Frank and try not to cry as he kissed me tenderly and then with growing passion. Finally, I fall asleep with my cheek resting on Frank's chest, reassured by the rise and fall of his breathing.

The next morning, we hold hands at the breakfast table, and Edward says a prayer for Frank and Samuel. Hugs, tears, and many reminders follow the prayer. Mabel and Edith bring out a metal box filled with ham sandwiches, apples, cookies, a chunk of cheese wrapped up in waxed paper, crackers, a thermos of coffee, another Thermos filled with water, with cups for each man.

Uncle Edward shakes hands with Frank and Samuel and talks with them quietly.

Finally, the men climb into the cab, wave, and drive off with my heart.

Edith puts an arm around my shoulders. "We're going to keep busy while they're gone, Marie. You'll see. The good Lord will watch over them."

She gives me a motherly hug, and I thank God again for having found a second mama. We watch as the little girls wave and wave and call goodbye. When the truck house is out of sight, Julia sighs, and I fear we'll all burst into tears.

Uncle Edward turns to walk to the bank. He notices Julia and Jessie wearing new their dresses and shoes and tips his hat. "Well, have we been properly introduced? I didn't know we had such fine young ladies in the neighborhood."

The girls giggle, and I sigh, thankful for the distraction.

Jessie walks up to him and takes his hand. "I'm Jessie. You know me and Julia. Mama sewed us new dresses, and we bought new shoes."

"Did you? They're very nice," he says.

Julia says, "You're being silly," but she smiles now, too, and takes his other hand.

He gives them both a little squeeze of their hands. "See you later, girls!"

Aunt Mabel glances around. "I think my sister's right. We've got things to do. Let's go back in the house."

We troop back up the steps and into the house that is now our home.

The Jubilee Quilting Circle
Marie

"The country was in a bad way, and all the smart people that let this happen needed to get it fixed. President Hoover hadn't been able to get the job done. Could the new president do any better?"

~Edward Richardson

*O*nce we reach the kitchen, Aunt Mabel shows me the piece of paper taped up on the icebox with the address and phone number for the camp.

"I know it's hard to be separated, but this is the right thing to do for the girls," Edith says. "I'm thankful that Samuel and Frank are together and can keep each other's spirits up."

I nod, fighting tears, and clutch the keys to the old farm truck in my apron pocket. I head upstairs with the girls where I tuck the keys in the top drawer of the dresser next to Mama's jewelry box.

The girls want to play in their *playhouse*—their walk-in closet. I sit down on the nearest bed and watch them chatter back and forth with a doll and a teddy bear while I think about all the things I wanted to sew upstairs.

The Jubilee Junction Quilting Circle meets at Mabel's house now. They used to meet at the Methodist church, but Aunt Mabel jokes they got kicked out. They couldn't keep the quilting frame in place there from week to week, with other activities, so they started going to her house. The parlor has a large table perfect for a group of quilters, and there's plenty of room for the quilting frame on the other side of the room from the dining table. Right now, they're finishing up a Double Wedding Ring quilt to auction off to buy a piano for the church.

Aunt Mabel is excited about introducing us to her quilting circle. Edith and I help her lay out her tea set and slice up the chocolate cake she'd baked from a recipe printed in *The Jubilee Times*. It was a special Depression chocolate cake made without eggs, butter, or milk.

I'm a little nervous. The past week and a half had been quite a change from our days on the farm, with dawn-to-dust chores, laundry, cooking, and keeping an eye on the girls. I'd helped cook, clean, and sort through our things to figure out what to store. Soon, the girls had helped me fill up the dresser and bookcase.

My favorite room of the house is that sewing room in the attic, which is part of the turret. I thought I'd died and gone to heaven, with four stacks of fabric to choose from, and a bunch of patterns from the newspaper. I ended up making the girls three little dresses each, a nightgown, and an everyday house dress. I made nightgowns for me and Edith, and one for Aunt Mabel. And then Aunt Mabel gave me a pillowcase, which I filled with scraps from those dresses.

Edith and Mabel praised me and said I was working too hard. I should sit down and rest, listen to the radio or read a book, but I wasn't sure what to do with myself. Eventually, I found a book to read and started writing letters to Frank. I spent time with little Jessie, working on her letters and numbers, and Julia sat with us and read and wrote stories for her daddy. I need to see about enrolling them in school.

I helped dust the house and mop the floors for the gathering today. Edith had baked her famous chocolate cake. My mouth was watering just thinking about it, and I wonder how long it has been since the girls had eaten anything so fine.

They miss their daddy and grandpa, but they are the happiest I have seen them in a long time. This morning, the girls dressed up in one of their new dresses and kept twirling around in my bedroom, where I had a mirror on the back of my closet door.

"You did a real fine job on those dresses," Aunt Mabel says, coming into the room with some laundry.

Edith follows and agrees. "Marie's a talented seamstress. She can make just about anything with that fancy Singer machine of yours. My old Kenmore gave out last year, so it's been some time since she got to sew." She was sitting on one of the chairs at my little table watching the girls, wearing a dress her sister had given her. My mother-in-law's face is soft and relaxed, her hair fixed the old way, with some curls.

"We look pretty!" Jessie declared.

Julia agreed. "Thank you, Mama and Grandma and Aunt Mabel." We walk downstairs.

The girls have their play corner downstairs with a small table we found up in the attic with four little chairs and a toy tea set. Mabel said she'd saved the toys and furniture for her grandchildren, but since those daughters of hers hadn't given her any grandchildren yet, we might as well use it. Julia has her doll, and Jessie holds her teddy bear and promises they'll be well-behaved during our meeting.

Edith and I are wearing new dresses, too, from Mabel's closets. I think Edith looks pretty, and she tells me to enjoy my new dresses. "Those daughters were a mite spoiled, if you ask me. You look beautiful in mauve."

I realize I am nervous about meeting Aunt Mabel's friends. *What if they had seen us in our old shabby clothes?*

The first ones to arrive are Ginny Nelson and her sister Verdeen, and Ginny's two young daughters, Grace and Violet. Both girls aree pretty and sweet spirited. The older one, Grace, looks about eleven years old; her little sister, Violet, maybe nine. They see my little girls and walk over to say hello and ask if the tea was any good. Pretty soon, the four of them are chattering away and laughing. Jessie crawls up on Grace's lap, and Julia ran to get her favorite book to read with Violet. I relax.

Right off, I see that Mabel and Ginny are the best of friends from their hug. Mabel introduces her sister Edith and then me, and Ginny and Verdeen are both friendly.

Ginny says, "Welcome to our quilting group. We lost two ladies who moved away, so it's good to have you here, even under these circumstances. We heard about your family losing the farm. I'm so sorry. I see our girls are getting acquainted."

Her sister, Verdeen, says, "Now that FDR's in office, I hope we can get this country back on its feet. Too many good people have lost their homes and farms, and people are lining up for soup."

Verdeen knew how to speak her mind, and I like her immediately. Before I can say anything else, the doorbell rings, and two more women come in. I'd already met the preacher's wife, Mildred, a warm, funny, and very spiritual person. She comes in, hugs me, and says, "Marie, it's good to see you again. Oh my, that dress is lovely on you. And your girls look so pretty. Mabel said you made those dresses?"

A young woman named Helen slips in the door behind Mildred. I know she is the schoolteacher, and she looks about my age. She is smiling at my daughters.

"There's only a few weeks of school left, but we'd love to have your daughters join us," Helen says.

"Well, thank you," I say. "I imagine they would like to do that. My older girl, Julia, is smart and knows how to read and do math, but Jessie is only five and just learning her letters and numbers, you know?"

The girls smile back at Helen as she sits down to talk to them.

Sixteen

Meeting the Ladies in the Sewing Circle
Marie
"I see one-third of a nation ill-housed, ill-clad, ill-nourished."
~President Franklin D. Roosevelt

The doorbell rings once more, and when I open the door, I see two women talking and laughing.

"Now, Henny, really. Squirrels?" The shorter woman laughs, while the taller woman tries to adjust her oversized bag. They come in, still chattering, and Aunt Mabel approaches and hugs them both.

The shorter woman turns out to be Irene O'Connor, whose son James is the editor of *The Jubilee Times*, our weekly newspaper. Henny complains squirrels are stealing her newspaper and attacking her with acorns when she tries to retrieve it.

Henny, short for Henrietta, lives nearby in another Queen Anne. She is quick-witted, and I like her right off, too. She is tall and thin, with her gray hair piled up on her head. She wears her glasses a little necklace that hangs down on her chest, and there is a kindness in those sharp old eyes, I am sure.

Mabel, Edith, and I serve tea and cake, and we visit for half an hour before getting down to business with the quilting. The pink quilt is almost finished. It is beautiful and someone will be lucky to get it. Done in the Double Wedding Ring style, it will fit a full-size bed. As we chat, Ginny laments, "We're running low on fabric for the next quilt."

Aunt Mabel gazes over at me and smiles. "Marie here has sewn some dresses, and we'll take those scraps and start a Crazy quilt. What do you say, ladies?"

I ventured, "I've got an old pillowcase full of little pieces of fabric that I've been saving."

Everyone else around the table smiles. "Well, I got a little pillowcase full, too," admitted Mildred, and everyone else gets excited because they, too, have pillowcases full of fabric pieces.

Irene leans forward. "Yes, I'll look around."

Ginny asks, "Do you think we'd have enough for a whole quilt?"

Daddy had been a preacher before he passed. I think of his favorite parable and smile. "It's like the Bible story, isn't it? The loaves and fishes that Jesus blessed and used to feed the five thousand? The little boy shared his lunch and there were baskets left over."

I smile and look around the group. "If we put our scraps together we'll have enough for a quilt."

Edith speaks up, "I have a few things that I can cut up."

Henny nods. "I'll go home and look around. I think I've got some curtains that need to be replaced." There is a glint in her eye.

Irene jumped in. "Now Henny, don't start cutting up all your curtains. What will your poor son say?"

The rest of the women laugh while Irene explained to me and Edith that Henny's son was a fine young lawyer in town, with a sweet wife and baby boy.

Mildred murmurs, "Loaves and fishes. I love it, Marie! Isn't that what most of us are doing these days? Taking all the scraps that are left over and trying to make something beautiful." She smiles at me, and Edith's eyes fill with tears.

So they work on the pink quilt while I go to check on the girls. Grace and Violet had taken some pieces of paper and had the little girls color simple designs and they were putting together a paper quilt. Aunt Mabel got them some adhesive tape and put down a newspaper.

"Look what we did, Mama!" said Jessie. "We quilting too."

Helen comes over and we talk more about the girls and school.

Mabel says she'd asked Helen about it but wanted the girls to feel settled in here before we introduce more change.

I could tell she was being tactful. Maybe she didn't want me to have sent the girls in their shabby little flour-sack dresses, but maybe I was just being too sensitive.

We agree that I'll walk them to the school tomorrow and get them enrolled.

Verdeen takes another look at the girls' dresses. "You did an excellent job with those little dresses. I never enjoyed making clothes that much, but I love to quilt. Do you mind if I tell a few women about you? Lots of people would rather hire someone to sew a dress than make a mess of it themselves. What do you charge?"

I stare at Aunt Mabel and Edith. "I've never made clothes for someone else and charged money for it. I wouldn't know how much to charge."

Verdeen looks at me kindly. "Don't sell yourself short, Marie. You're a fine addition to Jubilee Junction and our quilting club."

Seventeen

Holiday Lights & Cookies
Gracie

"One of the most glorious messes in the world is the mess created in the living room on Christmas Day."

~Andy Rooney

David and Alex finished decorating the front of the house, and David's father was right. The outdoor lights were very festive and not at all overwhelming. We turned down the offers of a life size Santa, sleigh, and reindeer that could go up on the roof. We also turned down a row of giant candy canes. Our display wouldn't endanger any power plants, but it was done.

Mom and I had driven over to David's family's hardware store a few days earlier. We bought a wreath for the front door, a nativity set for the fireplace, ornaments for the tree, scented candles for the dining room table, more snow globes, and festive pillows for the couch. The interior looked very festive, overall, and the smell wasn't bad once you got about six feet away from the tree.

Agatha was avoiding the Christmas tree, probably because of the smell. She sulked in her cat tree. David surmised she was plotting her revenge. She seemed a little freaked out by the Christmas tree, taking a wide circle to stay at least six feet away. Our plan was working, perhaps too well.

To tell the truth, Agatha wasn't the only one avoiding the tree. I'd go put a gift in the tub, put the lid back on and scoot the tub back a little further away from the tree. I wondered out loud if I'd overdone the squirts of vinegar and was afraid my gifts would absorb the smell.

David laughed, but I noticed he was also keeping his distance. He suggested we experiment next year with just tin foil and orange peels.

We were baking sugar cookies today at Mark and Kathy's house, our favorite place to gather as a family. I hurriedly got ready and met him in the garage.

We talked about our two families' holiday traditions on the way over. Both families' traditions included drawings for names of family members to buy gifts for one person. Both also included events with our churches and communities, giving back and doing something for those less fortunate.

"I'd like to find something special that we can do each year to make our own family tradition," I said.

He nodded. "Me, too. Let's think about it and talk more later tonight."

Both Uncle Vern's truck and my dad's SUV were already parked in the driveway. Mom welcomed us at the back door, and we smelled the first batch of Christmas cookies baking.

Kathy waved us in as she took a baking sheet from the oven and put it on the top of the stove. "Just doing a sample batch to find out if my dough is firm enough." She gestured to the pan. "I don't want to add too much flour. My grandma always said to chill the dough and not to add too much flour."

David stepped closer and sniffed. "Nothing like the smell of Christmas cookies right out of the oven."

I was right behind him, nodding. "They smell and look great, Kathy, and here are three more cookie sheets to help, plus a roll of parchment paper."

Mark came into the room. "Cookies done already?" He grinned as he came up to Kathy and pretended to grab her spatula.

Kathy laughed. "Okay, Mr. O'Connor, I get the hint. Gracie, grab some napkins."

After a sample cookie, we got to work. Katie came in with a laundry basket and set it aside, then began mixing up another batch of cookie dough. My mother followed with another laundry basket. Twins go through a lot of onesies, apparently.

We established a system of someone rolling out the dough, others cutting out the shapes, and baking, then decorating. Someone else then made another batch of cookie dough to put into the refrigerator. Even the grandfathers helped, especially with sampling cookies and watching the twins, who woke up from their nap and needed a diaper change.

My mom started mixing up her famous chocolate chip cookies for some variety. She used a mix of dark chocolate and milk chocolate chips.

Mark and Ken went out to do chores.

Dad and Uncle Vern sat and drank coffee, murmuring. Dad came over to talk to me and David about Uncle Vern keeping his promise. He's visited Jimmy Joe three or four times and updated his daughters by phone. Uncle Vern also reached out to the Judge, asking for permission for Jimmy Joe's daughters to visit during Christmas week.

According to Vern, Jimmy Joe confessed how much he missed his wife and his grandson. He admitted he may have gone too far with his white supremacist talk and opened up to Uncle Vern about his grandfather and father's prejudice against minorities. Jimmy Joe felt tremendous guilt for not supporting Shirley and protecting his daughter-in-law and grandson, and for not telling Billy the truth about his parents. Vern brought the pastor to see Jimmy Joe at his last visit, and the pastor prayed with him and promised to come back.

My father shrugged. "I've always respected Uncle Vern, but he surprised me. I was angry with Jimmy Joe for putting my family in danger, but Uncle Vern saw beyond that man's racism to see a person full of regrets. Mark checked Ancestry and our third great-grandmothers were sisters, so Jimmy Joe is our distant cousin. Uncle Vern says that good came out of something that could have been terrible and quoted Romans 8:28, "And we know that all things work together for good to them that love God, to them who are the called according to his purpose.""

David nodded. "I agree, Matthew. I was furious with that old man and his grandson, but I've always admired your great-uncle. Good for him if he got through to Billy Joe."

I wasn't ready to heap praise on anything that would make me forgive Jimmy Joe. Apparently, my facial expression gave me away, because Dad looked at me kindly. "It's alright, Gracie. You need some time."

"I'd better get back to the cookies," I said.

Mom, Kathy, and Katie were working steadily, rolling out dough, using cookie cutters, putting trays into the oven, taking them out of the oven, and onto cooling racks.

Uncle Vern sat beside Aunt Maggie, watching the twins in the family room. Dad and David walked over to help, snagging a couple of sugar cookies on their way. There were several baskets of freshly dried laundry nearby and they began folding towels, washcloths, and baby clothes.

"Gracie, you gotta see this!" David called.

I was packing cooled cookies into containers and glanced over at the family room.

Felix has retreated to his cat tree, watching the twins like he's at a tennis match, and I had to chuckle because there's a lot of action to see.

The twins are trying out some new walkers that are entertaining for us, but they aren't very efficient for getting somewhere. Sophie scrunched up her face in concentration, then her little feet danced on the floor, and she scooted maybe six inches. Sean grunted and scooted right past her. She looked startled and danced some more. So we had a floor show. Naturally, the iPhones came out, and we got some great shots.

After I'd filled four large Tupperware containers, I grabbed my notebook, and we went over our plans for our holiday meal when Kathy got a phone call.

Kathy stepped away to take it and looked excited. I heard her repeat, "Loaves of bread and fish? Hmmm. Mom? It's your cousin Janice."

My mom was busy dropping her cookie dough onto cookie sheets. She looked up at the mention of 'loaves of bread and fish.'

Katie talked with her cousin for a few minutes while we watched the babies, munching on some cookies that broke and trying not to grab another one. Kathy finished her cookie, got us both a short glass of milk, and then evaluated the babies' progress.

Felix pounced down to watch the twins more closely. They tried to inch closer to the cat, who backed away.

Uncle Vern laughed at the antics.

Kathy joined him. "They won't be running away from home any time soon."

Katie walked back to the table, excited, phone in hand. Her cousin found an old cardboard box from their grandma down in the basement and said she would bring it to us tomorrow on her way to her in-laws' house in Prairie Falls. She discovered an old Bible and a piece of quilt fabric with lovely drawings of bread and fish on a bookmark, and other stuff in there we might as well look at and keep if we're interested.

I looked at mom and repeated, "Loaves of bread and fish. Does that sound familiar?"

She frowned. "We need to ask Aunt Violet...."

We divided up a few cookies to take home, but we still had four large Tupperware containers with cookies to be frosted and decorated. Mom and Kathy reminded us of the sides we're making for the family dinner in two days. Tomorrow is Christmas Eve.

A noise caught my attention. I looked over to see Sophie scoot towards Sean and babble something, and he scooted backward, babbling something, both clearly unhappy. If only we had a baby whisperer to translate. Sophie rammed into her brother's walker, probably by accident, and began wailing. Sean responded with an angry cry of his own.

The grandfathers intervened, and each grabbed a baby out of the walkers. Just like teenagers, the little ones fussed at losing the keys to the family car. Finally, the men left the room, my dad looking rather uncomfortable, to go change diapers together.

My mother glanced at Katie, and they smiled. I tried not to smirk at the idea of my father changing a diaper. I'm happy that he's using disposable diapers because no one will get stuck with a pin. What a bonding experience it's sure to be.

Eighteen

Settling into Jubilee Junction
Marie

*"I wondered what they had seen, on the road to Wyoming—
farm trucks by the side of the road, loaded down with all the
things one couldn't leave behind, hungry children sitting at the
side of the road, flat tires, and a look of weariness on their faces."*
~Edith Olson

Mid-May

Samuel and Frank had been gone for four weeks. Sure enough, they're working at Camp Fremont, near Fremont Lake in Wyoming. Apparently, when they drove up to the commander's office, he wanted to come outside and get a tour of their truck house and seemed impressed by their ingenuity. He hired them on the spot! They supervised construction of several buildings to house the men and another for a mess hall to feed them. The young men arrive next week. Frank and Samuel each earn $40 a month as supervisors, and $30 comes home to us. I told Frank that I would save most of the money he sent home. In our whole marriage, we've never had a steady stream of income.

Verdeen was good to her word, and Edith and I were taking in sewing to help earn a little bit of money. I have three dresses to make, and two more to take in. Mabel said we didn't need to worry about earning money, but I aimed to earn my keep.

"Aunt Mabel, you've done so much for us. The girls feel safe here, and they like their new dresses and going to school. They miss their daddy, but they understand how hard things have been. I just want to feel like I am contributing something here."

"Nonsense. I love having you all here. Those girls are just darling. You're family. I hated being alone in this big old house all day," she said.

The girls are at school, and Mabel came up to check on me. She looked around the attic and called me over when she found her old adjustable mannequin. Mounted on a stand, I cand see at once its value and begin moving it towards the sewing room.

"This might come in handy if you're going to keep sewing like this. I'd forgotten I had this. Here, let me help." Together, we carry it into the sewing nook and find a space for it.

"Thank you," I tell Mabel, and she shows me what she remembers how to adjust the size of the mannequin. Carefully, I adjusted it to the size of the new dress I'm about to work on.

Edith does what she can to help her sister, and the two sisters fall into a rhythm—cooking, or cleaning together. They love working in the garden together, weeding and watering. Then, they bring the vegetables into the kitchen, where one washes and chops up the garden produce and the other uses the veggies for soups, side dishes, and salads. We've had fresh dishes made with tomatoes, green beans, and squash. Together we've canned, pickled, and given away produce.

I try to give Mabel money for groceries, but she won't hear of it. "We have plenty. Use that for your girls or yourself."

The girls love going to school and making friends. Jessie is excited about learning her letters and numbers, because she wants to read like her big sister. Julia has made several friends and loves hanging around the school library, devouring more books than she has ever seen in her life. Our country school back home had been more limited in its resources. Most of the students were from area farms, and no one had store-bought clothing, so they wore their shabby clothing and made-over dresses.

I spend several days each week sewing up in the attic. There's fittings, the dresses to assemble, hem, and make the final adjustments. And always, I ask to keep the scraps for our quilt.

I'm uncomfortable taking money for sewing, but the women all insist, so I make myself a little bag for those earnings. I'm not sure what I want to do with it, but I'm determined to help someone with that portion. I also put aside some money for when Frank returns. Edward helped me open a savings account, and it is encouraging to see the amount grow week by week in my bank book. Edward says my money was safe in an FDIC guaranteed account. I hope he's right.

I sort through our boxes, and find all the old curtains, and several precious feed and flour sacks I was saving up. Edith brings me more, and we cut them up into strips, squares, and whatever shapes might fit on the fabric.

Three or four women stop by the house, say hello to Mabel, and hand her a pillowcase full of fabric scraps for the loaves and fishes project. One of them says Henny had been going door to door in the neighborhood, begging for fabric for our next quilt.

Mabel feels torn between being amused and scandalized, but Edith chuckles. Soon, all three of us are laughing. And the pillowcases are accumulating on the chair by the quilting frame.

Each night, I write to Frank and read his letters while crying in my room. I missed him, but he told me some truly awful stories from some of the men in the camp about the Dust Bowl, where they'd plowed under too many acres of ground trying to grow crops. That resulted in uncontrollable dust storms that swept over the plains. Frank wrote that FDR wanted people to plant windbreaks. His CCC program planted millions of trees to slow the wind erosion that caused the storms.

Frank described seeing old trucks packed with a family's possessions, heading west. Later, he and Samuel encountered some of those people stranded on the side of the road because of vehicle breakdowns. They stopped to help several families, and would have helped more, but they needed to report to the camp. They witnessed homeless camps, soup kitchens, and abject poverty in many towns in Iowa and Nebraska as they journeyed west.

The CCC tackled a variety of projects out west, Frank wrote. They planted trees, fought wildfires, built dams, roads, fire towers, and campgrounds. Crews built picnic shelters, cleared acres of dead trees, built swimming pools, and performed wildlife studies.

Every time I finish reading his latest letter, I wipe my tears. *I have a roof over my head thanks to my Uncle Edward and Aunt Mabel, plenty to eat, and two strong hands.* My heart aches for those who do not have a family to take them in during these hard times. I wonder how I can make a difference in this community, and I pray, *Dear Father God, help me find ways to reach out to those who need it. Amen.*

Nineteen

Christmas Eve
Grace

"Christmas may be a day of feasting, or of prayer, but always it will be a day of remembrance—a day in which we think of everything we have ever loved."

~Augusta E. Randel

Christmas Eve we'd gathered at Mark and Kathy's house, hosting both the Nelson and the O'Connor families, as well as the Daniels. My parents, Aunt Delores and Uncle Rich, and Ken and Katie helped. After enjoying a crock-pot buffet of three soups and some simple sides, we went to church.

After we'd settled ourselves into the pew, I looked over and saw Uncle Vern and Aunt Maggie greet two couples and sit down with them. When one of the men turned his head, I recognized him as Roger Jenkins, son-in-law to Jimmy Joe. There were several teenagers and younger children with them. Right before the service began, the door opened and in came Officer Ben Carlson and Jerome Johnson, a young Black deputy, escorting Jimmy Joe. As soon as they got settled, they removed the handcuffs. His daughters hugged him, and he cried quietly and shook hands with his sons-in-law.

I stiffened, and David took my hand. "It's alright, Gracie."

"I'm okay," I whispered. I stared at the man, surprised to see such a different demeanor. He seemed smaller, somehow, than the big man who'd planted a wooden cross, talked crazy about his relatives having moved to Kentucky before the Civil War, and rammed into

Mark and Kathy's farmhouse with his pickup truck. Actually, he'd claimed to be a long-lost distant cousin whose 4th grandma was sisters with our 4th grandma. Now he sat quietly with a daughter on either side as the choir sang "Angels we have Heard on High," "O Little Town of Bethlehem," and "O Come, All Ye Faithful."

Pastor Carlson welcomed all our guests, nodding at Ben and Jerome. We sang several of my favorite carols, including "Silent Night" and "Hark the Herald Angels Sing." Uncle Rich, an Elder, prayed, then the pastor read the account of Jesus' birth from Matthew and Luke. He talked simply about the circumstances of Jesus' birth, the two groups of visitors—the shepherds and the wise men—and the family's escape to Egypt. He reminded us of why the tiny babe was born, quoting "God and sinners reconciled" and "born to give them second birth."

"Jesus came into this world with a mission—to redeem mankind," Pastor Carlson reminded us. "Celebrate Christmas with your family. Enjoy the cookies, stockings, and gifts. But don't forget about why he came—don't keep the baby in the manger. He grew up, and he performed great works, healing people and gathering a group of twelve disciples. Then he died on the cross for our sins, paying the price for our redemption with his blood.

"So Christmas is really all about redemption, a rather old-fashioned word. When I was a boy, my mother gave me the job of taking her S&H Green Stamps and pasting them into little books. Anyone remember these? S&H stood for the Sperry & Hutchinson company, and they put out a little catalog of all the things you could purchase with green stamps. Mom got them at the grocery store, the hardware store, and a few other places and collected them in a little basket. Once or twice a month, I sat down to watch cartoons with a wet sponge and those Green Stamps and filled up books. When she had enough of the stamps, she could trade them in for towels, dishes, toys, and other items. One year, she got all our Christmas presents with Green Stamps, including a radio for me, a doll for my little sister, another radio for my father's workshop, and a new bedspread and iron for herself. Mom was redeeming those stamps, trading them for the things she wanted. It sounds like a lot of work, doesn't it? I sure thought so, sitting at the kitchen table all those Saturday mornings!

"Redemption is the act of purchasing something. But we don't have to sit around and paste Green Stamps into little books to get this redemption. We simply must ask for forgiveness and accept a gift of eternal life. Jesus paid for it on the cross. Now, let's bow our head for prayer and then close with a final hymn."

As soon as the service ended, Uncle Vern shook hands with Jimmy Joe and promised to visit soon. Then he stepped back, so Jimmy Joe could have a moment to say goodbye to his family. Ben and Jerome escorted Jimmy Joe out of the church.

His family surrounded Uncle Vern and Aunt Maggie and thanked them. My father walked up to the group and shook hands with the men. My mother followed with Ken and Katie. Both daughters cried and apologized, and the moms hugged them, of course. Soon Uncle Rich and Aunt Delores were there, greeting them.

Mark and Kathy hesitated. They looked at me. I was squeezing David's hand and not sure what to do. Mom looked over, and I nodded. The four of us followed to meet the family, though I still hadn't decided if I could forgive Jimmy Joe and Billy.

Dad was talking with Roger and his wife, Roselyn, and introduced us. Roselyn had been crying and apologized to Mark and Kathy, then to me.

"Daddy's been lost without my mom. He feels responsible for Darlene's death, James Junior going to prison, and now his grandson Billy going to prison. He was looking for someone else to blame. I did some work on Ancestry and found the Jubilee Junction connection several years ago. I'm sorry for thinking Roger could stop him from doing something so frightening."

I wasn't mad at Roger or his wife, and I felt compassion for them. We met her little sister, Roxanne, and her husband, Scott, and a lot of children.

My parents invited them all to Christmas dinner the next day so they could get acquainted. Uncle Vern and Aunt Maggie would be there, as would Mark and Kathy.

"We can't impose on you," Roselyn said.

"We have plenty of food," Mom assured them. "Really, it's alright. Uncle Vern and Aunt Maggie have already reached out to you, and it sounds like we're cousins."

Ken and Katie arrived with the twins. They'd volunteered to sit in the back today. Dad made the introductions.

David and I were driving to Prairie Falls to have Christmas dinner with his family, so we'd miss out on the festivities, but Mom, Kathy, and Mark would fill us in soon enough.

The pastor came over, greeted them, and chatted. He exchanged contact information with them and promised to visit their father.

When we returned from church, we gathered around Mark and Kathy's tree, which does *not* smell like apple cider vinegar. But it has lots of tinfoil wrapped around the base, with a few orange peels scattered here and there.

David and Mark looked at each other and grinned when Ken asked why there's so much tin foil—and what's with the orange peels?

Aunt Violet sniffed. "Gracie, honey, I swear you still smell like vinegar," and the story came out, and my entire extended family laughed with me. David admitted to finding the article and sharing it with Mark and Kathy.

Kathy giggled as she held Sophie on her lap. The little girl babbled something. "I didn't like the idea of spraying my tree with apple cider vinegar, so I skipped that step. Felix is staying clear of the tree so far."

Felix huddled up in his cat tree. I asked Mark, "Remember the Charlie Brown cartoons where Snoopy acts like a vulture up in a tree? Doesn't Felix look like that now?"

Several of us turned around and looked at Felix, who scampered off to one of the boxes on the cat tree.

We exchanged our family gifts. Every Thanksgiving, we draw a name out of a basket. We aren't supposed to spend more than $25. The young adults buy board games or *Star Wars* sweatshirts for each other. The aunts and grandmas knit scarves, bought holiday sweatshirts on sale, or once, found look-alike pajamas for the whole clan. Ken and Katie were here at Thanksgiving, of course, so they're now part of the drawing and enjoyed it. But we each draw just one name, so we only need to buy a single gift.

Aunts Maggie and Violet crocheted special washcloths for dishes and made homemade strawberry jam each year. They ignored the rule, and everyone got jam and washcloths, but we love them and their gifts.

We opened our gifts, and ate pie, while we played with the babies, in their cute little Santa's elves outfits. David got a new board game, *The Settlers of Catan*, while I got a new messenger bag with a set of mechanical pencils and a cute flash drive on a lanyard.

We brought out our cameras and cell phones and attempted to pose the babies on a blanket. Unfortunately, they were trying to crawl away, so it didn't go as planned. It looked like the set of a baby get-away movie.

Sophie had maybe three wisps of hair for a silly little hair clip but looked adorable. Sean was more skilled at crawling, but Sophie rolled over better. We put them in their baby bumbo chairs, Mark and Ken fastening the safety belts, and the twins relaxed and smiled for the cameras.

Aunt Violet chuckled. "Whoever thought of that little chair was pretty smart. But I don't remember the safety belt. My goodness. I remember driving to town with one of my babies sitting in a laundry basket in the backseat with the older children."

Aunt Maggie agreed. "You'd get arrested today, Violet, for what we used to do. But we didn't have all these wonderful devices."

Kathy said, "The safety belts are a new feature. There was a big recall of the Bumbo chairs last year. Babies were being set up on tables and chairs in them and then falling out! Fortunately, we got the new, improved chairs that came with the safety belts in place."

Soon, it was time to put the babies down for the night, and it took about four of us to do that, because they're just so darn cute. My mother, Katie, Kathy, and I gave them a quick wash up and diaper change and then got them into their Santa jammies. The rest of us left so they could get one last shot at breastfeeding. Meanwhile, we headed out to attack the mess, to find that others had already cleaned up, and were about to watch a holiday movie.

I sat down on the floor with some pillows and a blanket next to David and got comfortable. The guys wanted to watch *Scrooged!*

Fat chance! I grabbed the remote, selected the DVD player, and we watched the Christmas movie about Ralphie, who wanted a Red Ryder Carbine Action 200 shot Range Model Air Rifle. After watching that dopey movie 20 times you'd think I'd know the title! Everyone repeated the catchphrase: "You'll shoot your eye out, kid." However, with the twins down for the night, we whispered it. Watching this movie on Christmas Eve was one of our Nelson traditions.

I snuggled into my new husband's arms, and thought, *I'm married. I have a wonderful husband. We're living out in the country in a farmhouse. I got the best present for Christmas.* I sniffed and realized that Aunt Violet was right—I could still smell that apple cider vinegar on my hands... or was it in my hair?

David didn't seem to notice, and if he did, he was kind enough not to comment. Maybe total honesty is not always a good thing in an intimate relationship. David kissed my neck sweetly and whispered, "I've been thinking about our own holiday traditions. Let's chat later."

I nodded and snuggled deeper into his arms and covered us with one of the many small blankets kept in a large basket kept in the family room. When the movie ended, someone passed around a cookie plate, and several people got up to make cocoa. I munched a sugar cookie and got up to help.

Twenty

Loaves and Fishes
Marie

"And he asked them, How many loaves have ye? And they said, Seven. And he commanded the people to sit down on the ground: and he took the seven loaves, and gave thanks, and brake, and gave to his disciples to set before them; and they did set them before the people. And they had a few small fishes: and he blessed, and commanded to set them also before them. So they did eat, and were filled: and they took up of the broken meat that was left seven baskets. And they that had eaten were about four thousand: and he sent them away."

~Mark 8:5–9

Mid-May

A few days ago, Julia came home from school with a tear-stained face. "Mama? Could you make a dress for my friend, Sarah? She only has one dress to wear to school, and her shoes are old, and Sally said something mean to her."

Her eyes were full of tears, and I held her close for a moment because I could not speak.

Edith and Mabel walked into the entryway, to find Julia sobbing into my arms, and little Jessie started crying now, too. Mabel took Jessie into the kitchen and comforted her, while Julia and I calmed down.

Edith handed me a handkerchief and gave one to Julia. Julia and I blew our noses, and Julia told her grandmother about her new friend and the teasing Sarah was getting at school.

"Grandma Edith, I remember wearing my old dresses over and over. I didn't like it. I love my new dresses, and I want Sarah to be happy."

Aunt Mabel rang the town operator who put her through to Helen, the schoolteacher, on the phone, and told her about the situation. We invited her and Sarah's family over for a meal the very next night. Since the girls teasing Sarah had done it outside of the classroom, Helen hadn't known about it.

Helen arrived first and expressed her concerns and apologies. "Many of these children are wearing hand-me-downs or made-over clothing. But most of them have more than one dress. Children grow so fast it's hard to keep up with them. But Sarah has seemed so sad lately, and I didn't know why. Now that I do, I'm going to deal with the offenders."

Mabel shook her head and put an arm around the young schoolteacher. "Helen, you can't read minds. Julia said it was happening before school. But I have a feeling you'll come up with a lesson plan to address the matter."

Sarah's family arrived next. Sarah's mother, Hazel, was a sweet, scared young woman in her late 20s with three children. She told us her husband went west with his brother, looking for work almost a year ago. She looked down and admitted she hadn't had a letter from him since he left.

Edith and Mabel had cooked up an enormous pot of chicken, vegetables, and noodles earlier in the day, and the children were eating it up, and so was their mama. Helen came over earlier and helped set the table, and I realized she was lonely. She and I sat on either side of Hazel. Julia sat by her friend and told her they could have seconds and even third helpings.

There was a knock on the door, and in came Henny.

"Is there some sort of meeting going on here tonight that I forgot about?" she said, looking puzzled. I realized she was probably watching our house from her front porch.

Mabel said. "Sit down and have some supper with us."

So Henny did just that.

Edward and Henny engaged the young mother in conversation,

while Helen and I took the children one by one into my upstairs sewing room. I got their measurements, writing it all down. First, Elizabeth (Betsy), 12. Next, Sarah, 9, and David, 5. Finally, I escorted Hazel upstairs for her measurements. Her eyes got big when I explained what I hoped to do.

After Hazel left, Henny wandered into the sewing room, where I sat looking over my notes. I had a stack of fabric beside me, and I was looking at the lists. I had asked each child for a favorite color.

Henny gave me a hug. "This is so sweet of you, Marie. How are you able to do this, making clothes for someone just because your little girl asked you to? You aren't getting paid to do this work, you know."

"I can't just sit by and watch a little girl wearing one shabby dress to school, can I?" I asked. "Not when I have the means to do something about it. A few weeks ago, that's the shape I was in, along with my girls."

"I don't want to hear any fussing from you," she muttered. She dug in her pocketbook for a hankie and came out with a five-dollar bill. She pressed it into my hands. "For your sewing supplies."

Later that day, someone from church brought over some extra fabric they had, and then others did the same. We received sacks and parcels of sewing supplies at our door almost daily. I had been busy sewing clothes for hire and sewing clothes for our Loaves and Fishes work, and now I was low on fabric, thread, and buttons. Within a few days, all my shelves were full again.

"It's like the loaves and fishes," I murmured, as I cut out the dresses. Then I thought of another scripture my mother liked to quote: *Cast thy bread upon the waters,* from Ecclesiastes. She used to tell us to be generous and share what we had with others, and one day we'd be rewarded.

We sewed three summer dresses for the girls and mother. Mabel, Edith, Henny, and Helen helped hem the dresses and add buttons. Edith and I took our little stash of money from sewing, and we bought socks, shoes, and underwear for Hazel and her children. I sewed two pairs of denim pants, two pairs of shorts, and three short sleeve chambray shirts for the little boy. I made pajamas for the two little ones and nightgowns for the mother and her older daughter, Betsy.

The quilters showed up to help hem the dresses, sew on buttons, and do whatever they could to help. We take over the dining room and table for the day and soon it's organized chaos.

"Say, we got any more brown thread?"

"How does this hem look?"

"Pass over the scissors, please."

"I need the button jar."

"Marie, you did such a great job—and thank you everyone for coming over to help. Hazel's going to be so happy." Mabel dabbed her eyes before getting out the cookies she'd baked and making tea.

The next week, we invite the family over for supper again, and give them their clothes, having them each try on an outfit. Henny and Helen join us for the meal.

One by one, the children go up to my bedroom and put on one of their new outfits and then come down to the dining room to show them off.

We start with Sarah, who loved her new blue dress. Julia inspects her and smiles. "You're so pretty, Sarah!"

Hazel cries. "I don't know how to thank you. I've been feeling so alone. My mother is caring for Grandma Shirley in Kansas City. My in-laws are in Nebraska, and they haven't written or called in six months or more. They lost their farm and have their own worries, but they haven't seen the children for almost two years. I don't have any other family here."

Pastor Martin Jones and Mildred drop by for dessert. As he talks to Hazel, we find out where they're living. Hazel and her three children are crammed into one room at the Jubilee Boarding house, and she admits her money's almost gone. Her husband left them there after they lost their house and business, and he hasn't written to them or sent any money since. She doesn't know where he is or how to reach him. She's been cleaning houses to pay rent and feed her children.

Henny's face shifts from listening to Hazel's story with compassion to expressing consternation. "Well, you can't stay there! Listen here, I have a nice large house next door, with three bedrooms that I'm not using. Why don't you all come stay with me? I'm sure we can find some things for you to do to help me out. I'm getting on in years and can't keep house the way I once did. You'd be doing me a big favor."

Hazel hesitates for only a moment and then accepts. Every woman in the kitchen needs a moment with a hankie, which any decent Christian woman has in her pocket. We make the arrangements on the spot.

Pastor Jones looks around the table. "We'll be there around four o'clock. And I'm going to talk to the owners of the boarding house. Is it possible that there are others staying there who need our help?"

Pastor Jones and Mildred meet us at the Boarding House with a few cardboard boxes, and we pack her up, not that she has much. We get her moved in with Henny, where Hazel will have her own bedroom. The older daughter has a bedroom, and the two little ones will share a room. They are all delighted. Henny is strutting around, having a fine time, settling them into their rooms.

We find out that Hazel is an excellent cook who knows her way around the kitchen. Her Mama taught her to make biscuits that are to die for, and her homemade apple pie is wonderful, with a flakey crust made from lard and apple filling with cinnamon. Betsy, her older daughter, 12, is a hard worker ,and the two youngest children are thriving. Henny and Hazel fit together like a long-lost mother and daughter, with Hazel somehow disarming Henny's sarcasm with her gentleness.

Laughter fills the Queen Anne next door. When Henny's son visits, he finds the house clean, his mother cheerful, and home-made apple pie cooling in the kitchen. He tries to hire Hazel as his mother's housekeeper, but Hazel said she can't take the money because she and her children are living there, and that they should pay rent. Henny winks at her and bargains with her son to pay Hazel $30 a month.

Julia is thrilled because her new best friend, Sarah, lives next door now. Her other best friend was Grace.

Mildred, Mabel, Helen, Hazel, and Henny talk about it all over tea. We determine to discuss the situation at the next quilting meeting.

Hazel has joined our group. She's out in the kitchen with Edith and Mabel dishing up a pie. Everyone else is in the dining room.

Ginny asks, "Are we overlooking our purpose here? We're quilters, but shouldn't we also be looking around for the folks who need help?" She turns to me. "Marie, you have a gift. I've seen no one who can measure someone, adapt a pattern, and get it cut out and put together so quickly."

Mildred agrees. She says, "Edith said it the other day when she told me you have flying fingers, my dear!"

I am pleased but uncomfortable with their praise and protest, "But you all helped with hemming and buttons and collecting sewing supplies. I couldn't have done it alone."

Verdeen declares, "We're a good team. Let's help other people. Surely in these hard times, there are folks in need."

Ginny adds, "Yes, all we have to do is just look around. Henny, how are things going with Hazel and her children?"

Henny beams. "Hazel and I are getting along real well. You know, I missed hearing children's laughter in the house. I feel like I have a purpose, and I'm not just some old lady watching the squirrels play in the trees out the window. I agree with Verdeen. There must be other people who feel alone, who need a little encouragement and maybe a nice new dress?"

Verdeen looks thoughtful. "But we wouldn't have known about Hazel's dire situation without little Sarah. We need help to gather information."

We recruit Helen to be our spy and help us find other children who need shoes or clothing at school. Mildred vows to be on the lookout for other families like Hazel's, separated by these hard times, struggling, and in need of our help.

I've discovered my purpose, and I write Frank all about it in my next letter. I know now how I can help others—with my flying fingers, sewing clothing.

Twenty-one

Christmas with David's Family
Gracie

"Christmas is the day that holds all time together."
~Alexander Smith

When we got home, David and I celebrated Christmas Eve by our tree, still undisturbed by Agatha, who sat in her tree and pouted. I scooted the tub clear of our stinky tree and opened it up, hoping the contents didn't all smell of vinegar.

I'd gotten David a new Christmas sweater, some cologne, and his own leg lamp from *The Christmas Story* movie, as well as several books. He grinned.

I looked up at the cat tree and Agatha. I held up a new cat toy, a rubber mouse, and Agatha jumped down with the stealth of a jungle cat. She grabbed the toy from my hands with her teeth and raced back to her perch, looking at the Christmas tree with what I thought was derision.

David sniffed. "I guess she can still smell that apple cider vinegar."

We laughed and kissed. Then he handed me an extra-large gift bag. Inside, I found a warm robe in jewel tones, matching bootie slippers, three fancy notebooks, gel pens, and a small box holding a tea mug with a saucy saying on it.

"I love it!" I said, slipping on the slippers. "Thanks."

"I love the leg lamp. Should we find a place for it down here?" he asked.

The next morning, we got up early to go spend Christmas with David's family.

We filled our travel mugs with coffee and tea, and grabbed a few cookies to tide us over. I'd already loaded the back seat with gift bags and three pies.

I glanced up at Agatha, still perched up in her cat tree, and told her to be good. She seemed to sneer at me, but I might have imagined it.

On the drive, we compared ideas about how to create our own holiday traditions.

David said, "I don't think we need to stress about it, Gracie. We can choose things we like to do together, whether it's going ice skating or making popcorn and watching a holiday movie."

I nodded. "Yes, I guess I am stressed, trying to figure out if there's anything left for us to do. After all, we inherited a lot of holiday traditions from both families. Movies, gift drawings, making cookies, and going to church on Christmas Eve."

"So, let's keep talking, and if we don't figure it out this Christmas, there's always next year, right?"

We had barely parked at his parents' three-bedroom ranch house when two small people were standing in the doorway, waving.

David's little brother, Alex, and father, Harry, came out to the car to help. Alex took the gift bags and handed his father the large bag with the pies. His father grinned. "Three pies? Let me put those in my workshop where they'll be safe! Thanks, Gracie."

Daisy and Jack were jumping up and down as we came into the house.

We took off our coats and kneeled to their level.

David and Jack pretended to wrestle. Daisy and I danced while singing "Jingle Bells."

Then we greeted the adults.

David's Mom, Ruth, laughed. "They've been waiting there for twenty minutes. We were debating what to do if you didn't arrive soon."

Joanna hugged us both. "I said, throw them out in the snow."

The children looked up and shrieked with laughter as their mother picked up Daisy and started for the door. She hugged her and put her down.

Her husband, Jared, grinned. "I understand you have some wonderful outdoor lighting. We're going to drive over and check it out, so leave it up for a while."

David nodded. "Yes, we love it. Very festive. Come visit and we'll give you the grand tour. That was so much fun. Thanks, Dad, and Alex."

Alex shrugged. "I was a little bummed that you nixed Santa and the sleigh for the roof."

We enjoyed a simple breakfast of egg and sausage casserole, cinnamon rolls, fresh fruit, coffee and tea, and orange juice.

After cleaning up, we went to the tree and opened gifts.

His family did a drawing, too, but we always brought the kids a present, even if it was just a few books or toys. One rule: No guns, toy or otherwise!

Afterward, we cuddled on the couch and watched a holiday cartoon with the children, Joanna, and Grandma Ruth. Jared and Alex went downstairs to watch football with Harry.

Daisy and Jack cuddled up between us, with their little blankets, like two little puppies. Daisy leaned into me.

"I like to cuddle with you, Gracie. You smell nice," she said, thus relieving my fear of still reeking of vinegar! I'd showered long last night and again this morning.

"Back at you, Daisy. You smell like baby shampoo."

The cartoon ended, and Ruth recruited us to help clean up the debris from the gift exchange. I collected gift bags to be reused—we'd split them up and use them again. David collected all the cardboard and plastic from the packaging torn up to get to the gift itself. We'd take them to the recycling center.

The children took a few of their new toys to their playroom at Grandma's house, and Joanna followed with a cardboard box. They were giving away a few of their older toys. Otherwise, grandma was afraid their toy box would explode. The children seemed skeptical but filled the box.

While they sorted out toys with their mother, we talked with David's Mom, Ruth, who asked, "So what quilt are you two researching these days?"

We told her, and her face lit up. "I love Depression-era quilts because they're so creative. People did great work with limited resources. I hope you'll send me pictures. It's amazing what those women accomplished with so little. My Grandma Ethel and aunts used to tell us stories. Those were hard times, alright. Many families lost their farms and had to ship off kids to relatives all over the Midwest. My grandpa was fourteen and ended up in Wisconsin with a cousin."

David nodded. "I told Gracie about him."

I said, "That's awfully young to be away from your family."

"They didn't have a choice. His folks couldn't feed the family after they lost the farm. They had eight kids, I think. The six older ones had to grow up too fast, I'm afraid. That's how Grandpa became such a great dairy farmer."

I asked, "Did they have any stories about the farm sales and foreclosures?"

"Yes." Ruth thought a moment." My grandparents talked about how awful it was for farmers. Families watched their friends lose their farms, went to farm sales, cried together, tried to hang on, and it seemed hopeless. Banks failed, and it sent shock waves into the communities. Bankers were often the leading citizens. Farmers got desperate and worked together and saved a few places, but it was a big mess. Tenant farmers were the most vulnerable. Some small farming communities never recovered."

David and I glanced at each other. We'd driven through small towns that seemed left behind or hollowed out.

His mother continued, "Some of our grandparents avoided banks after that. My great-aunt shared a story about finding hidden money in her mother-in-law's house after she passed away. Her mother-in-law hid money in books, behind picture frames, and even in a coffee can under the bed. Women tried to make do with what they could find. They planted bigger gardens, made over an old coat, used flour and feed sacks to make clothing or towels, took in sewing, or did anything at all to keep food on the table. Men in the country hunted, of course, and almost everyone canned food and made home-made jams and jellies."

David leaned forward, listening. "Of course, I always read about the great migration west during that time. Did anyone talk about that with you?"

"Yes. Remember, the 1918 Spanish flu hit the Midwest, and then the Dust Bowl and Great Depression devastated them again, just a few years later. Families lost their homes and farms, and many headed for California. Some of them found a place to settle down along the way, and others made it to California, of course. Many stayed out there because they needed workers for the war effort. I had an uncle and aunt who did that. They left for California in the 1940s and came back about a decade later."

David regarded his mother with respect. "I think I'm not the only historian in the family."

I nodded. "Yes, it is good to hear that, Ruth. Family stories help us understand these historic events. Somehow, when you're in school, reading about the two World Wars, the Great Depression, and the pandemic of 1918, you don't think about how it impacted your family."

We chatted about other things, and David told her about the progress of his book project. But I kept thinking about her comments about the family stories of the Great Depression and the hard times.

Later, we enjoyed a simplified version of a Christmas dinner. Turkey, a slimmed down corn casserole, green beans, a fruit platter, and mashed potatoes. No rolls, despite the concerns of sacrilege. Our splurge was the pie: we brought no-sugar apple, pumpkin, and lemon chiffon.

David's father, Harry, had been diagnosed as prediabetic. So we were all trying to help.

We stayed until 8. The children were drooping when we said goodnight.

As we left, I hugged Ruth, and she whispered, "I hope you solve your mystery. I'm sure you will, Gracie."

When we got into the car, I checked my phone for messages and found half a dozen texts with photos of our new extended family. Mom saved the best for last.

Call me when you get home. Important update on family drama.

I didn't wait. I told David, "Something's up with Mom." I called her and put it on speaker phone.

"Hey, Mom. We're on our way home. Had a great day and see you did, too. What's going on?"

"Gracie, I'm so glad you called. Remember Jimmy Joe's wife, Shirley? The older daughter was going through a box of her mother's things recently and found a letter from her mother that Jimmy Joe was to give to Billy. It urges him to turn away from violence and tells him the whole truth about his parents and the reason his father is in prison. She included a couple of photos, including one that shows his poor mother's face after a beating and one that shows her holding Billy when he was a toddler, shortly before she was killed."

"James Junior went into the military right after high school and got in with some White supremacists. They went to fight in the First Gulf War in 1990, and his unit was part of the ground assault. They captured prisoners and apparently went beyond the Geneva convention, torturing them. He was dishonorably discharged, along with several others in his unit.

"So, she made a copy of the letter and photos. She wants to visit Billy and give him the letter. She thinks the appeal from his grandmother may make a difference and save him from repeating his father's mistakes," Mom said.

"That's a lot of detail and possibly high drama," I said, sitting up. "It could go horribly wrong."

Mom agreed. "Yes, she has been agonizing about it. I told her about what we'd learned about the power of family secrets to divide and cause problems. It could go wrong, but it could also give him the answers he's looking for."

"What does her sister think? Does she support Roselyn's plan?"

"Roxanne is not sure what to think. She's a worrier and doesn't want to be there, so I volunteered to go with Roselyn."

Of course she did. My mother could have been a hostage negotiator.

"Be careful, mom! When are you going?"

"I'm not sure. Roselyn must call the prison and make the arrangements. I'll let you know how it goes."

David looked at me after I said goodbye to Mom. "So, that's intense. From White Supremacist wanna be to an orphan whose mother died from abuse and father went to prison. I thought nothing could make me see Jimmy Joe sympathetically, or Billy either. But there's always a story, isn't there?"

I settled back to enjoy the rest of the drive and chat with David. But I was eager to hear what happened at the prison when Roselyn and Mom go to visit Billy. Roselyn had found a letter addressed to her nephew, answering his questions about what happened to his parents. How would he respond? Would he be able to process this very traumatic news?

Twenty-two

Murder at the Bank
Marie

"A slow, silent fear had set in. It was a new kind of mass fear, never before experienced on a national scale. It was a fear about losing everything—jobs and savings, homes, farms, ears, children."

~John Wilkinson

Late May

$\mathcal{U}$ncle Edward came home looking shaken. He sat down in the parlor and put his hands over his face. When I first saw his face, I thought he was ill.

The girls aren't home from school yet, so he's early.

Edith and Aunt Mabel walk into the room. When Aunt Mabel sees him, she stops and says, "Oh, Edward? What happened?"

He struggled to get it out. "It's Thomas Jenkins—the bank manager in our Prairie Falls bank—a farmer came into the bank today, and shot him on the spot without saying a word. The sheriff has the farmer in custody, poor wretch. We foreclosed on him last week, and he was in a blind rage. When they went to do the farm sale, he refused to let people go onto his land. He had a shotgun and a brother and uncle with shotguns. People have gone mad!"

He takes a big, shuddering sigh. "I drove up and took charge. There were all kinds of witnesses. I'll spare you the details, but several clerks fainted. It was all very shocking and gory. I have seen nothing like that horrible scene since I was in France during the Great War. They're coming into the building to clean tonight, and we'll reopen the branch by the end of the week. But I must go visit his family this afternoon. Jenkins was a young man and had a young family, including a baby."

My mother-in-law fetches a glass of water for Uncle Edward, shaken as he recounts the horrors of the day. He accepts the glass and drinks it down.

Aunt Mabel stands there with a sad expression. "I wonder if they've got family around here? I'll call Mildred and find out if the pastor knows about it yet."

They leave the room, and I stare at Uncle Edward, trying to think of what to say.

"I'm so sorry," I say at last, feeling inadequate. "This has been a terrible year for everyone. But remember, you've done something good for us. You got Frank and Samuel those jobs, and you've given us a home here. This isn't your fault."

He looks up at me. "Thank you, Marie. I wish I had one of your pillowcases over there, full of money. I'd buy up all these farms. It's foolish to foreclose on a man for a few hundred dollars when he's poured his lifeblood into the soil. I hate this whole situation. For the first time in my life, I don't want to get up in the morning and go to the bank. I used to love it, but now I dread it."

I've seen my uncle with his bottle in the basement once or twice when I've taken down some laundry or had to grab something down there. I've seen the toll the foreclosures have had on him and watched the tender way my aunt looks at him. He looks at me sadly again and stands up, trying to put himself back together. I lean over and straightened his tie and pat his arm.

Before he and Aunt Mabel leave to visit the family, I say, "I wonder if they need any clothes for the funeral, at least the mother? It wouldn't take long to make a black dress."

Mabel nods. "Yes, I will check with his wife and pass on your offer."

Uncle Edward and Aunt Mabel visited the distraught young widow whose parents were there. My practical aunt went to work, putting together a list of meals to be delivered to the family.

When they returned, Uncle Edward said he would go back tomorrow and help the pastor and his wife with the funeral arrangements. He'll make sure the bank supports the widow with some income. He looked grim when he said this, and I think he's aged in the past few months.

Aunt Mabel takes me aside and tells me that the widow would appreciate help with a dress. Her parents will watch the children so she can come over for a fitting later this afternoon. We go up to the sewing nook and look at patterns and fabric and realize we don't have any black fabric. So she makes a phone call. About an hour later, Mildred, the preacher's wife, shows up with a small bolt of black fabric, black thread, and some buttons.

We pick out two different dress patterns to show the widow.

Mildred thanks me. "This is wonderful of you to do, Marie. We appreciate your flying fingers."

"I'm happy to help, but it's such a sad situation. Uncle Edward said the farmer was remorseful after the fact, but that doesn't help a young wife with little children."

She agrees, then she and Mabel leave on an errand to pick up more fabric.

When the girls came in after school, Edith and I greet them and gave them their snack. They leave the kitchen to wash up, chattering about school, and my mother-in-law and I glanced at each other.

"Should I say something?" I ask.

"No, they're children," she replied. "They don't need to know all the wickedness in the world. They'll find out tomorrow at school, no doubt. Let them have one more night of good sleep."

The girls finish their snack, and then go to play in their room, where the closet is a reading nook, and they've inherited a toy box from the attic.

An hour later, there is a knock at the front door. It is the young widow, still looking rather shell-shocked. Edith welcomes her in, and we take her upstairs to the sewing room, where we had laid out two patterns, the fabric, and several kinds of buttons. My measuring tape, pencil, and small notebook are waiting for us.

She picks the pattern and buttons and then bursts into tears.

"How can I worry about looking nice for my poor husband's funeral?" she wails. "I'm too young to be a widow. My children need their father. I need my husband!

Fortunately, Aunt Mabel and Mildred come into the room. They embrace her and let her have a good cry. I sit down at the little table, looking at the measurements and calculating how much time I need to complete the dress.

Suddenly, I'm nauseated and put my hand on my stomach. I haven't been feeling well for more than a week. I shift on the chair and try to focus on my task at hand.

Edith looks at me sharply, "Marie, is something wrong? You don't look quite right." She moves toward me, but I wave her away.

"I'm alright. I must have eaten something that upset my stomach."

She replies, "I don't think you've eaten enough for a bird in the past couple of weeks. What's going on?"

I shake my head, but Edith stares at me in a rather appraising fashion.

The widow composes herself, apologizes, and turns to me. "I don't know how to thank you," she says.

Mildred and Mabel wait for her at the attic stairs.

"That's alright." I stand up, walk over to her, and put a reassuring hand on her arm. "I'm so sorry for your loss. I'll let you know when you can come back, and we'll do a fitting to be sure it's alright."

I turn back to my work to pin the pattern against the fabric, and suddenly, I'm quite lightheaded.

Aunt Mabel and Edith catch me before I tumble down, and sit me down on the chair by the worktable, still unsteady. Mildred and the young widow turned back to stare at me.

Mildred asks, "Are you alright?"

"I'm fine. I just had a touch of lightheadedness there. So sorry to alarm everyone," I tell her and blow out a deep exhale. "I need to get to work."

Mabel looks at Edith. "Please stay here and keep an eye on her. I'll see our guests to the door."

Edith watches me like a hawk as I lay out the pattern, cut the fabric, and get to work on the dress.

When Mabel returns, she looks first at her sister and then at me.

"Marie, are you pregnant?" she asks.

I straighten up. "Pregnant?" I repeat.

Edith looks happy and excited, but I falter, put the fabric down, and swallow hard.

"I'm taking you to my doctor tomorrow," Mabel says. "I think we're going to have some exciting news for Frank and Samuel."

I don't know if I want to laugh or cry. I'd love to give Frank a little boy and the girls a brother—or a sister. *Can I be pregnant?* I think back.

"For now, let's not talk about this with the girls." I say. "And to answer your question, well, I haven't had my monthly cycle since well before the move."

I turn back to the dress, determined to get as far as I can.

Behind me, Edith nods in agreement. "Yes, I think that is best. Oh my, Marie. A baby! If it is true, it's wonderful news." She gives me a small hug, gets a chair, and sits down not far away.

Mabel agrees. "Wouldn't that be a special surprise for Frank? I'm going to start dinner."

Edith says, "We'll be down shortly."

I keep working, pushing the idea of pregnancy aside, like surplus fabric that I would deal with later. Within the hour, I cut out all the pieces, assemble the dress to sew it, and go downstairs to help with supper. My stomach rebels, and Aunt Mabel hands me the canister with saltines. I eat a few of them, but only nibble at supper.

I gaze around the table. Uncle Edward is listening to the girls chatter about school, and smiling. He enjoys the antics of the little girls. I think he wants grandchildren.

Aunt Mabel and Edith are like peas and carrots, fitting together. We've become a family. I'm thankful to be here, but I miss Frank.

I put my hand on my stomach. *Can it be true? Am I pregnant?* I count the months on my fingers under the table. The baby would be born around the holidays—in December. A Christmas baby! My eyes fill with tears, and I brush them aside, pretending to eat my supper.

Across the table, Aunt Mabel smiles tenderly.

Edith, sitting beside me, puts an arm around my shoulder. "We're all here to help, Marie. You aren't alone. You're family."

114

Back to Work
Gracie

"None of us had much back then, but we had each other, and we could quilt and talk."

~Mabel Richardson

As soon as I could get Mom alone, I looked at her expectantly and said, "So, are you going to tell me about your visit to the prison?"

She grinned. "Yes, it went well, I think, considering all the emotional bombshells. We got to visit Billy in a small conference room, complete with a guard at the door. His aunt hugged him and introduced me. Then, after a few minutes, Roselyn handed him the letter from his grandmother, telling him she found it recently and thought it was high time he knew the truth.

"He read it slowly and looked at the pictures. He asked his aunt, 'My dad beat my mother to death when I was a little kid? I always wondered why he was in prison. And why my grandparents got so tense when I asked questions. They said my mother left, which made me feel like there was something wrong with me.'

"We stayed a few more minutes and then our time was up. Roselyn thanked me for going with her on the way home. We went back to the B & B and debriefed her sister and the whole family. Everyone felt relieved to have the secret out in the open. Now, of course, someone needed to tell Jimmy Joe the news."

After Christmas, we got back to work on the Crazy quilt mystery. David and Carl dug into the museum archives and found pictures of Samuel's truck house along with a newspaper clipping. Some notes attached included a sketch of the interior and an interview in the spring of 1933. The truck house belonged to Samuel Olson, brother-in-law of Edward Richardson, the local banker.

Charlotte and I went back to the Special Collections room. We found several oversized plastic boxes. We hit gold when we opened the second box. Inside, we found a set of 11 x 14 photographs of quilts auctioned at the Jubilee Junction Methodist church in 1933. I recognized the pink Double Wedding Ring quilt that belonged to my grandmother Grace. I'd been told that her mother, Grandma Ginny, loved it so much she had the top bid.

As I flipped through the photos, encased in plastic, I noticed the Crazy quilt, and then—was I seeing double? A second Crazy quilt. There were photos of the pastor with different women and children, including two women holding up a quilt. Finally, a group of smiling women stood by a new piano, so it seems the quilters' work was successful.

Charlotte and I took the photos upstairs and compared them to Katie's album and then scanned them as well. I wanted to compare the pictures of the women and show them to Aunt Violet, just in case she recognized anyone else. Great-Grandma Ginny, her sister—Aunt Verdeen—and someone named Mabel had already been identified.

David found additional articles in the newspaper archives at *The Jubilee Times*. They included one about a church quilting group that used their quilts to raise funds for a church piano. We've identified several people in the pictures:

The banker's wife, Mabel Richardson.

The preacher's wife, Mildred.

The schoolteacher, Helen.

Mabel's neighbor, Henrietta (Henny).

Grandma Ginny and her sister Verdeen.

At the heart of the group is a lovely young woman who smiles as she helps hold up the Crazy quilt.

At her side is a sweet looking older woman who seems focused more on the young lady than the quilt.

Katie identified those two women as her Grandmother Marie and Great-Grandma Edith. Edith and Mabel were sisters. Edith and Samuel lost their farm, and their son, Frank, and his wife, Marie, were farming with them.

Charlotte and I looked at the databases again. We looked for 1933 and banks in Jubilee Junction and surrounding towns. We found an article about Edward and Mabel who lived in the big Queen Anne I'd always loved as a child. They had four children, all grown and scattered across the state.

It was time to examine the contents of the box that Katie's cousin had dropped off, and to ask Aunt Violet to tell us her story.

Loaves & Fishes
Marie

"If you share what you have with others, you may find that just like the loaves and fishes Jesus used to feed a crowd, you'll have more than enough."

~Marie Olson

Late May

$\mathcal{T}$rue to her word, Aunt Mabel arranged for me to go visit the town doctor the following day. Afterwards, I'm in a state of wonder because—I'm pregnant! We agree not to share the news outside the family before I can tell Frank.

However, the two women continue to hover as I'm sewing the dress for the widow. I'm not used to being monitored.

Edith makes sure I sit down and put my feet up twice a day. Mabel has me drinking some special peppermint tea that is good for the tummy, and it's helping control the nausea so I can eat more.

Finally, the dress is done. The widow comes to try it on, and thank goodness, it fits. She leaves with the dress, thanking us.

Then we turn our attention back to the Crazy quilt. I tell the quilting circle we should work on the front side, but we've barely started.

We dump out half a dozen pillowcases onto the dining room table and sort them into piles by color. Then we lay out a full-size muslin sheet and examine our piles of fabric scraps. I selecte shapes and move them around, finding a pleasing arrangement of shapes, colors, and patterns. Fascinated, Edith and Mabel hand me possibilities. I lay them into place, reject some, move them around, and sometimes swap them out. After an hour, we take a break. Edith and Mabel follow me, using small pins to attach the pieces in place.

We have a quick lunch, then go back to work on arranging pieces of fabric.

In the meantime, Helen has found three more children needing clothes, so we put the quilt aside. I sew pajamas, dresses, pants, and shirts, and the members of the quilting circle join in adding buttons and hemming things up.

Mildred is making a list to go shopping for shoes, socks, and underwear. She hands me a small change purse with coins and a dollar bills. "A few people wanted to help with that next shopping trip," she confides.

Several other people have hired me to sew a dress, a skirt, or alter clothing. I'm thankful for the work and for the chance to contribute. Although every time I try to give Aunt Mabel money for groceries, she hands it right back for my "loaves and fishes" fund.

The sisters work together out in the vegetable garden and tend to the rhubarb, blueberries, and strawberries. There are three mature apple trees and a cherry tree that supply them with fruit for jelly and jam.

I realize that while my aunt and uncle aren't wealthy, they are kind and generous people. My aunt has been lonely since her daughters married and moved away. After the years apart, with Edith busy out on the farm, the sisters were happy to be together. With us here, Mabel and Edward are happy to share what they have, and my heart is full of gratitude.

After five days, we have the layout for the front of the Crazy quilt. The quilt group will help us secure them and add batting.

By ones and twos, our friends in the quilting circle stop by, mouths gaping at the sight of the Crazy quilt.

"It's beautiful!" Mildred gapes. "I didn't know a bunch of scraps and leftovers could be so pretty."

We lay down a new muslin sheet and begin work on the back side. I dump out a few more pillowcases full of scraps and get to work sorting them by color and repeating the process. It takes four or five days, but at last we're done. Or are we?

Edith finds six more bags of scraps that were dropped off and put in the front hall closet.

We get more muslin and repeat the process with new pillowcases. We take a break to eat a sandwich and drink some tea. then we finish the second side of the second quilt. This takes several more days, and our backs are aching and our fingers are numb. But when I look at my Aunt Mabel, she is smiling through her tears. "Loaves and Fishes," she says.

Edith finds several more pillowcases in a corner, so we dump them out on the dining room table. We smile as we marvel at the sight. How can there still be leftovers? Then I remember the disciples gathering up all the leftover loaves and fishes after everyone had eaten their fill.

I have an idea, so we go up to the attic and look around. We find a brown paper sack full of cotton batting. We use the pillowcases as our base, add some batting, and create a small Crazy quilt pillow for each member of the quilting circle.

We smile as we work because we've exceeded our hopes. As the next few weeks pass, we work on the first quilt, and I ponder how the new baby will fit into the family. I haven't told Frank yet because I have always waited until three months to announce the news, and I want to do the same with this pregnancy. I debate between telling him in a letter or sending him a telegram. I can't imagine telling him in a telegram.

But very time I think about writing a letter, there are dishes to wash, a dress to sew, or donations of fabric and buttons to sort out and organize. Then one morning, the sisters are working out in the garden and the children are in school, so I have the house to myself. I sit down at the table in my room and start writing a letter to Frank, telling him about the shooting at the bank, and everything else going on—including almost fainting, and Edith and Mabel catching me, and Mabel taking me to see Doc Carlson.

You're going to be a daddy again, Frank, I write.

When I'm done, I find an envelope, copy the address from Frank's last letter, and sit back and stretch. I can imagine his face when he opens the letter and reads about the pregnancy. I can hear his voice. Before they left, he said, "I love you, Marie, and I'm going to miss you and the girls. I will miss holding you every night in bed. Please take care of yourself."

I go downstairs to find a stamp and walk to the store to mail the letter. The mailman picks up the letters there every afternoon. I felt emotional about telling Frank the good news, and when I arrive back home I have a good cry, then go back to work upstairs in the attic sewing room, taking advantage of the natural light. When it get darker, I am thankful that my aunt and uncle had gotten electricity several years before.

Edith, Mabel, and I work on the pillows. When they're done, we'll hide them away as a surprise for our sewing circle. We have just a few scraps of Crazy quilt fabric left—little portions that were stitched together but proved too small for another pillow. We'd gotten a lot of varied fabrics from calico to cotton from garments to feed sack and flour sack fabrics used to create clothing.

I have another idea. I find some pretty pieces of cardboard and create a set of bookmarks for everyone, with a little scrap of fabric, two loaves, and three fishes, plus the year. *Loaves and Fishes, 1933.*

When hope seems lost for so many people, I feel gratitude for the abundance of love in Jubilee Junction. Edith, the girls, and I have made new friends and reconnected with our family. I've found my purpose and we've been able to help people. Meanwhile, our girls are flourishing in the school here and making friends. And we're slowly building a nest egg for later, when the men return from Wyoming.

I wonder, what does God have in store for us down the road and how will this baby change our lives?

Twenty-five

What's in the Box?
Gracie

"Our hearts grow tender with childhood memories and love of kindred, and we are better throughout the year for having, in spirit, become a child again at Christmas-time."
~Laura Ingalls Wilder

We gathered at Mark and Kathy's farmhouse and stared at the large cardboard box that Katie placed on the table. Someone had scrawled a name on it in pencil: Marie Olson.

David is taking a video of us doing an inventory of what is in the box.

Katie grinned. "I've been waiting to do this."

We sat down, and she emptied the box.

Kathy handed me a notebook and a pen—she's well-trained. I removed some cotton gloves from my purse and handed one pair to Katie and I put on the other pair. Then I asked for two tea towels. Kathy handed me the towels.

Katie took out a worn Bible with a bookmark, which I lay aside.

Old family Bibles often have names recorded that are useful for genealogy searches, and I opened it to check if someone had written in family names, and they have. Carefully, I placed the Bible on a tea towel, then picked up the bookmark and admired it. A scrap of the Crazy quilt sewn to a bookmark. *Loaves & Fishes, 1933, Jubilee Junction.* I admire it and snap a few photos.

We pulled out:

A faded little calendar from 1933.

A small notepad and pencil with a list of measurements for a black funeral dress, size 10.

A small pillow, covered with Crazy quilt patches.

Some letters tied up in string.

An old-fashioned jewelry box.

The Good Housekeeping Woman's Home Cookbook by Isabel Gordon Curtis (1909).

An old pillowcase with a dozen scraps of fabric inside.

I opened the calendar and note a list of the quilters' names on an inside page.

Quilt Circle, 1933.

Mabel

Mildred

Henny

Helen

Edith

Irene

Marie

Hazel

Katie looked transfixed at the sight of the little pillow, and reached for it, just as we heard a little gasp, and Aunt Violet sat up straighter, saying, "Loaves and Fishes. . . I remember now!"

She dug in her pocket for a handkerchief and sat for a moment, lost in her thoughts, with tears trickling down her cheeks. Mom quietly took Aunt Violet's hand to comfort her, and Katie passed over the box of Kleenex.

Finally, Aunt Violet spoke. "Mama always took Grace and me to the Quilt Circle meetings at Mabel's Queen Anne. Vera didn't like to go because she hated sewing, so Mama let her stay home. Mabel was my mama's best friend. Her sister and brother-in-law had lost their farm to foreclosure. So, Mabel's sister, Edith, and niece, Marie, came to stay with Marie's two little girls, Jessie and Julia. Their daddy and grandfather traveled out west in that truck house to work with the CCC. Edith was such a sweet woman, and Marie, her daughter-in-law, was more like her daughter. Marie loved to sew clothing for people in need. She came up with 'Loaves and

Fishes' because whenever we ran low on fabric, someone would drop more off, and the shelves would fill back up."

Aunt Violet looked off into space. "It's been so long since I thought about those days. Of course, I was just a little girl back then. Oh, my goodness. Look at that sweet little pillow."

And then, she told us the rest of the story.

Twenty-six

The Crazy Quilt Auction
Marie

"Sure must be a great consolation to the poor people who lost their stock in the late crash to know that it has fallen in the hands of Mr. Rockefeller, who will take care of it and see that it has a good home and never be allowed to wander around unprotected again. There is one rule that works in every calamity. Be it pestilence, war or famine, the rich get richer and the poor get poorer. The poor even help arrange it."

~Will Roger

June

The first Crazy quilt is done, and it's beautiful. Ginny took it home to work on some final touches with Verdeen. While it's there, young James O'Connor visited and took photos of the Crazy quilt on her antique bench.

He also came to one of our quilting sessions at Mabel's Queen Anne, took pictures of us, and did an interview.

We're thrilled about the upcoming church event, where we'll auction off the Crazy quilt to raise funds for a new piano. The quilting club had already presented the pink Wedding Ring quilt to the church, but its sale hadn't raised enough money. So we're going to auction off the Crazy quilt and then enjoy a potluck lunch.

Pastor Jones asked Uncle Edward to handle the auction, since he's the banker and has done auctions before.

Finally, Sunday arrives, and we're all in our Sunday best dresses, but I realize the waistband is getting tight on my stomach. I really need to sew a few maternity dresses or let out some seams. Resting my hand on my belly, I smile just as Julia walks into my bedroom.

"We're all ready, Mama," she says, staring at my hand on my tummy.

I pretend to adjust the waistband and buttons. "Wonderful." I pick up my pocketbook, and we go downstairs where Jessie is twirling around to show off her dress to Uncle Edward.

He claps.

Aunt Mabel has wrapped the quilt up in a sheet with Edith's help. I glance over at the second Crazy quilt, still on the quilting frame. It's coming along nicely.

Then we get into Uncle Edward's car and drive to church.

My tummy is still a little off, but the tea I'm drinking is helping.

When we walk into church, we are greeted by the ladies in the quilting circle.

Hazel and her children walk by, and she says hello. "Oh, my goodness, Marie. It's gorgeous!" She stares at the bundle. Mabel has unwrapped it and is showing it off, and soon there is a crowd admiring it.

I smile at Hazel. "I didn't do it alone. Everyone helped." Then I lean in a little closer. "You look good, Hazel. Henny has treated you kindly?"

Hazel grins. "She's been wonderful. We get along real well. The kids love her and call her Grandma Henny."

Henny is talking to Edith and my aunt, and when she turns, she smiles like I haven't seen her smile before. Hazel and her children have brought joy and companionship to her as well as purpose.

Soon it is time to sit down and begin the service, with lots of enthusiastic singing, clapping, and plenty of *Amens!* punctuating the air. The old piano was almost falling apart, but Miss Lavonne makes it sound good. We sing three hymns, the offering plate is passed, there is a few announcements, and the preacher offers a hearty prayer for all of those who could not be here today.

Jessie wiggles a little beside me, her little hand on the quilt bundle. She whispers, "It's real pretty, Mama."

Rev. Jones looks around the sanctuary and notices a bigger than usual crowd. He speaks about the Beatitudes, from Matthew 5:3–12. Today's verse, verse 5, *Blessed are the meek: for they shall inherit the earth*. After about twenty minutes, he switches topics from what it means to be meek to money and steps down from the platform with the altar.

"I suppose you think you're going to buy the Crazy quilt tonight. Well, I hope you brought plenty of cash money because we want to get our new piano. Sister Mabel and Sister Marie, would you bring the quilt up here so we can show it off properly?"

I blush, but Mabel nudges me, so we slip out of the pew and take the quilt upfront. We unwrap it first, and the preacher grabs the sheet and lays it on the front pew. There is a hum of comments from the audience as we hold it up and then turn it around to show the other side.

The preacher says, "I've been hearing a lot about this quilting group because Mildred belongs to it. They've begun helping others who are struggling during these hard times. These women have taken the lesson Jesus taught us about pooling our resources to meet people's needs. And word has gotten around. People started dropping off their extra fabric, buttons, and thread so the group could create clothing for people in need. And this lovely quilt results from all those discarded scraps of fabric that you ladies save in pillowcases. God took those loaves and fishes and multiplied them, and here's the result!"

Uncle Edward slips out of the pew, bringing a small wooden box with him for the money. He nods at the preacher and starts the bidding.

My arms aree getting a little tired, but I glance over at Mabel, and she is standing tall and proud. It gives me some courage, too. I shift position and relax. This is better.

The bidding goes on and on until it reaches $100.

Finally, the gavel goes down, and the quilt is sold—to Henny.

She comes up to the front, looking triumphant. Henny opens her big pocketbook and counts the dollars into the box, while Rev. Jones and Uncle Edward smile. She takes her quilt, which we'd just folded up for her. We're standing there with Henny, wrapping the sheet around the quilt, when everything goes crazy.

A young man walks up the center aisle with a shotgun, aiming it straight at Uncle Edward's head.

"I'll take that money, thank you," he calls out, as calm as anything.

Hazel jumps up from her pew and out to the center aisle. "Henry J. Sullivan, what are you doing here?" she demands. "And where is your worthless brother—my husband?"

Hazel walks up to face him, shotgun or no shotgun. She is fearless.

The audience gasps as Aunt Mabel and I exchange frightened glances.

Henny stared at Hazel in a mix of alarm and admiration.

The man with the shotgun ignores Hazel at first and then turns to her, swinging the gun away from Edward momentarily. "He ain't coming back, Hazel. He's done with you." He turns back to the preacher, who is now standing beside Uncle Edward. "Well? Where's my money?" He snarls and lifts the gun. "Guess I gotta start shooting people, but I'm walking out of here with that cash box." He shifts and aimed his gun at Hazel, who has followed him to the front of the church.

Rev. Jones holds his hands up in a conciliatory manner. "Now, son, put down that gun of yours and let's talk. You don't want to shoot up my church or hurt that sweet little woman. Maybe we can work things out."

The young man is sweating. I think the rest of us are sweating, too. I feel frozen. Only the preacher and Hazel seem calm.

The young man shifts to address the preacher, with the gun still aimed at Hazel. "I know what you're doing, preacher. You're stalling. It ain't going to work—"

He is interrupted by Henny dropping the quilt on the floor and aiming her sizable pocketbook at the back of his head.

The pocketbook wins, and Mr. Henry J. Sullivan is out cold on the sanctuary floor. The shotgun clatters to the floor after bouncing off a pew, discharging a round that just misses the preacher but hits the pulpit behind him.

Two deacons rush up to be sure we were all unharmed. One grabs the shotgun while the other kneels by the unconscious man.

"Pastor, he's breathing," he calls.

Henny rushes over to Hazel, who slumps and flings her arms around Henny's neck, and the two women weep.

Uncle Edward and the pastor exchanges glances and sag in relief.

Uncle Edward sits down, the money box on his lap. He is shaking.

The pastor looks out at the astonished congregation. He opens his mouth to say something and shuts it while he regains his composure. He finally gestures for Miss Lavonne to resume her seat at the piano.

The song leader jumps up and cries, "Sisters and Brothers, let us join our voices in praise as we sing 'Count Your Blessings.'"

Miss Lavonne bravely leads the way, with the song leader and the congregation joins in singing with a few people shouting "Hallelujah" and "Praise Jesus."

Mabel and I pick up the quilt, no worse for wear, refold it, and wait to give it to Henny.

Henny straightens herself up and so does Hazel, their arms still around each other. They find their clean handkerchiefs, which any decent Christian woman would have in a pocket, and blow their noses. Henny looks at me and Aunt Mabel and whispers, "Desperate times call for desperate measures and don't you ever underestimate the power of the pocketbook." Then she grins, like a naughty little girl, as we all sit back down and join in song with the congregation.

Twenty-seven

The Power of Henny's Pocketbook
Marie

"Desperate times call for desperate measures and don't you ever underestimate the power of the pocketbook."

~Henny Carlson

*A*unt Mabel and I stare at Henny.

We all sit down in the front pew, and she shows us the inside of her pocketbook—there is a small brick inside.

Henny whispers, "When you're going to have an auction and a there is going to be a box full of cash money, you might well expect a little trouble. As I was walking out the door, I grabbed the door stop. I could hear a little inner voice telling me I might need it today."

One of the deacons went for the sheriff, and he soon returned with a deputy to take Henry away just as the congregation wraps up singing the hymn. The would-be thief is still humbled by his encounter with Henny's pocketbook. He sits on the floor, rubbing his head, and complaining of being dizzy.

Henny looks down at him. "Young man? Wherever your worthless brother is, you can tell him that Hazel is doing well. She and the children are living with me now, and we will visit my son—a lawyer—for a divorce. She has *me* and our quilting circle, and this church, and she and the children will be fine." Hazel's three children came up front, and stood by their mother and adopted grandmother, staring him down.

Henry blinks and mutters something that we can't hear. The

deputy helps him up, puts the cuffs on him, and leads him out of the sanctuary to the applause of the congregation.

The preacher and Uncle Edward look both shocked and relieved. The preacher recovers his wits and jokes, "Well, no one can say the service was boring today, can they? Just the same, let's ask for the good sheriff to escort Edward to the bank, so we can get the money there safely."

Edward walks with the sheriff to the front doors of the church, followed by two board members.

We all breathe a sigh.

Henny turns to the preacher. "So, what's our total? Can we get the new piano yet?"

The preacher recovers, looks at his notebook, and says, "Well, look at that. Yes, we can! The Crazy quilt put us over the top."

People around us shout "Praise the Lord!" and clap.

As we were celebrating, we hear a gunshot outside.

Henny, Hazel, Mabel, and I run towards the door, Edith on our heels as well as the preacher and Mildred.

Once outside, I wasn't sure what had happened.

Someone lay on the ground, and there is a lot of blood. Suddenly, I don't feel so well and need to sit down. I collapse on the church steps, breathing hard.

Edith sits down with me. "Are you alright?" she whispers.

I nod.

Then, we noticed the details. Two people are wrestling in the grass, and one wears a deputy's uniform. A third person in uniform jumps into the fray and wrestles a shotgun out of the hands of the man on the bottom. The sheriff handcuffs that man.

In front of me, Hazel, Mildred, and Mabel are picking up dollar bills, five-dollar bills, and a few ten-dollar bills and putting them back into the wooden box that Henny holds. Hazel's children are running around, catching other bills as they scatter in the wind.

I avert my eyes from the body. Who had gotten shot? I look around and identified the preacher, the deputy and—I hear a man's voice from behind me.

"Marie, are you alright?" It is Uncle Edward. He'd been knocked to the ground in the fracas.

I nod, "Are you?"

"I'm fine," he says. He straightens his tie.

Aunt Mabel rushes over to hug her husband, not saying a word.

The sheriff comes over, a little out of breath. "You alright, Edward? I should have thought about an ambush, but I never expected him to shoot the prisoner."

His deputy has the ambusher in handcuffs, and I assume it is the ill-fated husband.

Hazel glances over at him, and he stares right back. She stiffens and turned away.

"Hazel," he calls. "I did it all for you and the kids, honey. I never told my fool brother to aim the gun at you. I wanted some cash money so we could start over. . ."

She didn't turn. "All this time and you never sent a dime. You never wrote a letter to let us know where you were. We'll be fine without you." Her face is tear-stained, but her voice is strong.

Having captured most of the money, his three children—Miriam, Sarah, and little David—turn their backs on him and move near Henny and their mother. It was clear where their allegiance lay.

The man sags in defeat and starts sobbing as the deputy and sheriff lead him away.

Hazel and Henny gather the children in their arms and hold them closely. Mabel, Edith, and I stand there, showing our support. Soon, every member of our quilting circle is standing there, encircling them, with the preacher and Uncle Edward joining us. We'd gained a member in Hazel. And Henny had gained a daughter. All of us marvel at Hazel's courage in standing up to her no-good brother-in-law, but she shrugs it off.

Fortunately, we'd recaptured $88 of the $100. Henny quietly reaches for her pocketbook and pulls out $12 to give Uncle Edward to deposit for the church. She turns to us and says, "I hope those dollars go to people in need. It'll be their lucky day, won't it?"

And that's the story of how Uncle Edward auctioned off the Crazy quilt to buy a new piano for Jubilee Junction's Methodist church. And if we thought that Miss Lavonne had made the old piano sound sweet, she plays the new piano with the biggest smile. Joy just spills out with that beautiful music and fills the church with praise.

Later, Henny added a little plaque to the side of the piano— *Compliments of the Jubilee Junction Quilters, Loaves and Fishes, 1933.*

Twenty-eight

Putting Together the Clues
Gracie

"The Greatest Generation was formed first by the Great Depression. They shared everything—meals, jobs, clothing."
~Tom Brokaw.

I took the family Bible and packet of letters to Charlotte, and we sat back down to look at genealogy sites. Within minutes, we had a family tree for Katie. The Spanish Flu, 1918–1920 left her grandmother, Marie, orphaned when both of Marie's parents and her only sister died early on. Confusion over a common first name had halted our search earlier. Now we had middle names, dates of birth, and other information, thanks to the old family Bible. We discovered that Marie's paternal grandparents died not long after the pandemic as well.

We found Frank, his parents Samuel and Edith, and his aunt and uncle, Mabel and Edward. Marie and Frank married when she was not quite 18, the same week her parents and sister died and were buried during the second wave of the Spanish Flu in 1918.

Charlotte looked up from her laptop. "We often talk about the Spanish Flu as if it happened in a season, but it lasted over two and a half years, occurring in several waves, starting in the Spring of 1918. The First wave began with mild symptoms. By the fall, the second wave hit, and it was the deadliest with higher mortality rates due to severe respiratory complications like pneumonia. The third wave began during the winter of 1918 and lasted into 1919. It killed many people but was less deadly than the second wave.

Outbreaks continued into 1920, but the virus faded. The global spread was made worse by WWI's troop movements and overcrowded conditions. Some estimate it infected up to 500 million people, or one in three people alive at that time, and it killed 20 to 50 million people."

I stared at her, trying to grasp those statistics. "I can't imagine that scenario, and especially without having the tools to fight the disease with. No vaccines, no antibiotics, not much of anything." Then I went back to my notes about Marie.

She and Frank farmed with his parents, living in a tenant house on the 250-acre farm. Samuel was a veteran of the Great War, but he had dreamed of farming and passed that dream onto his son.

Next, we found Edith's sister and brother-in-law, Mabel and Edward. Our search took us to more links about the Great Depression, banking, and foreclosures. Edward was a banker in Jubilee Junction. Edward was forced to foreclosed on sixty farms in Jubilee County, including his brother-in-law Samuel's farm. One distraught farmer murdered his branch manager after his farm went through foreclosure.

We looked more closely at Marie—it is her youngest daughter, Jessie, that is Katie's grandmother, after all.

Katie gave us permission to open the letters, read them, and scan them, so we did. They were love letters from Marie to Frank, and Frank to Marie, describing their days apart.

Marie's husband and father-in-law drove a truck house out to Wyoming to work for the CCC in 1933. They came back to visit when baby Jimmy was born over the holidays and then returned to work until the fall of 1935.

While Charlotte and I were busy, David was doing research on the CCC. He called us. "I reached out to a friend at the University of Nebraska at Lincoln because I remembered a paper he read at a conference about the CCC. Doug sent me some fascinating links about the CCC in the Great Plains. I always think of them working out west building trails, bridges, shelters, and structures in national and state parks. Many of those remain today even though the CCC ended in 1942 when America entered WWII.

But there are modern conservation corps modeled after the CCC on the state and local level.

"Not only that, the CCC, sometimes called FDR's tree army, planted over 220 million trees in a 1,300-mile zone, bisecting the Great Plains from Canada to Texas. FDR wanted to plant a 'Great Wall of Trees' to slow down the wind erosion that caused the Dust Bowl. The resulting shelterbelts were 100 feet wide and may have had up to 17 rows of trees, which provided shelter for birds and wildlife. Many of these shelterbelts still exist, Gracie! I'm a history teacher, but I didn't fully appreciate what the Great Depression was like before now. These stories are so important. We take for granted the work the CCC did 80 years ago, but much of it is still here, hiding in plain sight," he said.

While I was on the phone with David, Charlotte was scanning in and reading the letters from Marie to Frank. She smiled in triumph and put one letter aside. She discovered what the pillowcases full of scraps meant to the quilters of Jubilee Junction. They combined their pillowcases full of remnants, leftovers, and scraps and created two lovely Crazy quilts. Then they used the leftovers to create little pillows for each member for a keepsake.

I donned my white gloves and read the letter for myself. In the middle of our research, I got a call from Mom.

"Gracie, I have an update on Billy getting the news about his mother's murder at the hands of his father. I just got off the phone with Roselyn. Billy's suicidal now, feeling abandonment issues. He feels like his grandparents lied to him his whole life. They put him in the prison hospital because he was banging his head against the bars."

"Oh, Mom, I'm sorry."

"It gets worse. Roselyn and Roxanne had to come clean with their father. He was angry with Roselyn and hurt that she'd do such a thing, but then he broke down. Apparently, he promised his wife on her deathbed that he'd give her letter to Billy right away, but he didn't, of course. Now Jimmy Joe's a mess and begging to be allowed to talk to his grandson."

"What are you going to do?" I asked.

"I called Uncle Joey and Judge Carlson, and they're pulling some strings. We're waiting to hear from the prison. Roselyn and Roger are on their way to meet the prison chaplain and visit Billy. Pastor Carlson and Uncle Vern are on their way to Jimmy Joe. Just say a prayer, please."

"Of course, Mom," I managed. I disconnected the call, my thoughts swirling. *Now I'm supposed to pray for the two men who had harassed my family, threatened to kidnap me, and caused a ruckus at the courthouse?* I looked up and Charlotte was regarding me with kindness.

"What's going on now, Gracie?"

I told her, shaking my head. "So, now that we're third or fourth cousins and all, I guess I just ignore the past?"

My friend shook her head. "What they did was wrong and that's why they're in jail. Your mother and Uncle Vern have gone out of their way to help the family. It's tragic what happened to Billy, and his grandparents were trying to protect him but should have told him the truth as difficult as that would have been."

"Can you imagine growing up without your mother because your father killed her in a drunken rage? That's so messed up," my voice trembled as the words resonated. "Why is the truth often painful? My Great-Grandma Ginny didn't want to talk about what happened in California between her twin daughters either and it took six decades to reconcile Violet and Vera. The truth has a funny way of coming out in the end."

Charlotte still held the letter. "Read it for yourself, Gracie. Here's the story of the two Crazy quilts coming together from the combined pillowcases of a remarkable group of friends. Marie writes about finding her purpose in sewing clothes for people in need, and their loaves and fishes ministry. Sometimes the truth is beautiful—like a lovely old Crazy quilt."

I took the letter and read it with a smile while Charlotte scanned the next letter. The pieces were coming together. I only hoped my mother and Uncle Vern would be successful with their mission to help Billy's family.

Twenty-nine

The Crisis with Billy
Gracie

*"In these days of difficulty, we Americans everywhere must
and shall choose the path of social justice...the path of faith, the
path of hope, and the path of love toward our fellow man."*
~Franklin D Roosevelt

*D*avid and I had plenty to do to get ready for
the Spring semester, but it was difficult to concentrate. I'd finished
the afternoon at the library, thanking Charlotte for all her help
and packing up the letters and research. David met me at Aunt
Shirley's Cafe for an early supper and we compared notes.

David asked, "How are you feeling about this situation, Gracie?
Your mom asked you to pray for the man responsible for harassing
your family over the past year."

I thought about it. "I think I can finally see him as a person
who made mistakes and has a lot of regrets. I'm over the fear
and anger."

He nodded. "Good, because it looks like Uncle Vern and your
mother are determined to help."

We headed home and went to our offices to work, but I kept
checking my phone for a text from Mom about Jimmy Joe and
Billy. Finally, after two hours had passed, I couldn't stand waiting.
I called Mom, and she picked up right away.

"Oh Gracie, I'm so sorry. I was just about to call you." Her voice
was full of emotion.

"What's happening?"

"We're here at the prison. Give me a minute to step away. Roselyn is talking to Billy." I could hear voices in the background.

"Is Billy still banging his head on the bars?"

"No. He got to see his grandfather and talk—they arranged for a video call."

Pastor Carlson and Uncle Vern were with Jimmy Joe in Jubilee Junction, while Mom and Roselyn were with the prison chaplain and Billy an hour's drive away.

"Jimmy Joe surprised us all."

"What did he do?"

"He apologized to Billy for not giving him the letter right away. Jimmy Joe said it was wrong to let Billy grow up without the truth about his mother's death. He was afraid the truth would shatter the boy when he was much younger, even though Shirley kept saying that Billy needed to hear the truth from his grandparents."

"He told Billy that he was afraid of losing him. He'd lost Shirley and missed her every day. He'd loved his daughter-in-law, Darlene, and was ashamed that he lied and said she'd left on her own. Jimmy Joe has a lot of regret and shame, and he's being hard on himself. If only he'd listened to Shirley's pleas."

"He said he'd been talking to Jerome, one of the deputies who escorted him to court and church. He lost a parent to a violent death when he was a child and was raised by a single mother and his grandparents. Jerome's father was a young Black cop shot during an attempted robbery. Jerome encouraged Jimmy Joe to trust his grandson to hear the news and answer his questions."

"That's amazing right there. A Black deputy got through to him?" I said.

"Yes, he did. Apparently, Jerome was kind to Jimmy Joe as he brought meals or escorted him to meetings with his lawyer. But I don't think any of this would have happened if Uncle Vern hadn't gotten involved. So, Billy still has time to serve, and Jimmy Joe has his hearing after the first of the year. Their troubles aren't over, but they're both in a better state of mind. Roselyn brought a photo album with lots of pictures of his mother and has promised to keep visiting and telling him all she can about his mother and her side of his family."

"That's incredible, Mom. I'm guessing Billy isn't eager to communicate with his father?"

"No. He needs time to process the story of his mother's abuse and death. He's also dropping the White supremacy that his father espouses. He no longer wants to be like his father. Of course, we've already learned how secrets can divide and threaten to destroy a family. It almost destroyed this one, but Jimmy Joe's daughters are doing their best to keep that from happening."

"Thanks, Mom. Good job. I have to say that I didn't understand what you and Uncle Vern thought you could accomplish, but you did it!"

After we said goodbye, I went to tell David. I had a good feeling about Billy and Jimmy Joe. What did David say earlier? Everyone has a story, and once you know it, it's easier to have some compassion.

Thirty

Touring the Queen Anne
Gracie

"In the Great Depression in which I grew up and remember vividly, unemployment was over 25 percent, and over 35 percent where I lived. A grown man would work all day, 16 hours, for a dollar. I remember hundreds of people walking by, people who had come down from the North just to get warm. They would come to our house as beggars even though they might have a college education. People didn't have money. They bartered; they'd trade eggs or pigs. It was just completely different."

~Jimmy Carter

My mother had arranged for us to go tour the Queen Anne, taking family and friends along—Grandma Molly, Aunt Violet, Aunt Maggie, Aunt Delores, cousin Allie, Kathy, and Katie, plus Charlotte, Shelly, and Tiara. Great-Grandpa Patrick and the grandfathers volunteered to babysit the twins and told us to have fun.

The Queen Anne's a local landmark and the city council has talked about finding funding to restore it so they can do tours or rent it out for parties. Fortunately, one of Mom's cousins has the keys. We gathered on the front porch in anticipation.

Charlotte's delighted. "I've always wanted to see the inside. Thanks for inviting me!"

Shelly agreed. "Me, too! We've driven by this house my whole life. I can't believe I'm finally going to see the inside."

Tiara walked up to the window and peeked inside. "I think I see a big fireplace. I always wanted a mantel to decorate at Christmas."

Allie peeked into the heavy front door with fancy glass windows. "Me, too! Delores, didn't you have some big party here when you and Rich were dating?"

Delores grinned at her daughter-in-law. "You have a good memory, Allie. Yes, it was an after-prom party. It's such a lovely house, and there are several fireplaces."

Aunt Violet touched the railing. "I was here a lot as a young girl. It was the nicest house in town. I can't wait to see it again."

Grandma Molly smiled, "I'm curious, too. My sister-in-law's Queen Anne isn't as large and doesn't have an enormous yard. Of course, back then, they all had big gardens."

Mom's cousin, Susan, greeted us as she unlocked the front door. We walked into the Queen Anne and admired the lovely craftsman details, with the woodwork, arches, and sunny porches with glass doors. The foyer had polished walnut parquet flooring. We walked around the first floor and admired the spacious parlor where the quilters met, the large kitchen, and bathroom. There was also a library/sitting room in the back with ceiling to floor bookcases, tables and chairs, and old-fashioned horsehair couches. Then we saw the turret room, a small room on the second- floor landing. We walked upstairs to see the bedrooms, considered roomy in their day, and still very nice, with large closets. The windows had wonderful views of the neighborhood through the branches of the trees.

Violet paused in one bedroom, and her eyes lit up when she saw the closet door. She opened it up, peered inside, and chuckled. "This was our playhouse. When I came over to play with Jessie and Julia, we liked to take our books and dolls in here and play."

She smiled, and we looked around, ignoring the torn wallpaper and worn furnishings. I tried to see it through the eyes of Aunt Violet as a child.

We walked up to the attic. Mom and her cousin talked quietly while the rest of us wandered around. Finally, we all ended up in the sewing area tucked up in the attic above the turret room.

Mom's cousin turned to us. "This house is so interesting. The woman who lived here, Mabel Richardson, had a little sewing room with an old treadle sewing machine set into the turret. When the city acquired it, there was still some fabric in the shelving above the workbench. Someone found a little bookmark with two loaves and three fishes, 1933. On the backside, it said: "If you share what you have with others, just like the story of the loaves and fishes, you'll have more than enough."

Aunt Violet smiled and closed her eyes for a moment. She murmured, "Loaves and fishes … pillowcases full of scraps. When her stack of fabric ran low, someone dropped off more fabric, zippers, buttons, and thread. Marie would sew more clothes, and we'd gather up the scraps for her pillowcase. Henny went door to door in her neighborhood asking for fabric, and the members of the quilting group spread the word all over town to take leftover fabric and sewing supplies to Mabel's house.

"I can almost see Marie at Mabel's old treadle sewing machine. She made clothes for people who needed them. Your grandmother Marie was a good woman, and your mother and aunt were the sweetest little girls."

Katie and Kathy listened to every word intently. Katie reached out to take Aunt Violet's hand, and Kathy took her other hand, Aunts Maggie and Delores standing behind her, patting her shoulders.

I watched the three of them having a moment, looking away to gather my thoughts and wipe a tear or two. Allie, Shelly, and Tiara stood beside me, looking around.

Charlotte looked around the attic. "The city has owned this house since 1936? What have they done with it? Has it sat empty all these years?"

Susan paused. "They rented it out for teas and fancy parties for decades until it was getting too shabby in the 1990s. Gracie, your mother, Delores, and I had our graduation party here. Then more recently, they used it as overflow storage for the city—for old office furniture, old computers, and boxes of old files for the archives."

I looked around the room. "So why is the house empty now, except for a few pieces of furniture?"

Susan looked at my mom apologetically. "I didn't want to say anything. Becky called and asked if I could show you the Queen Anne, and I was happy to do so. I work in the mayor's office and hear a lot of gossip. Lately, there's been talk on the city council about whether to sell the property. Over the years, many developers have asked about the location from big chain restaurants to drug stores. We've always said no. But the house needs improvements and there isn't any money in the budget. The sale of this house and its grounds would help. Last week we got the work order to clear out the house, and I'm not sure why."

Mom spoke up, "And the city council would really sell the property to the highest bidder and let a developer tear down this property and put up... what? A McDonalds, dollar store or sub shop in the heart of historic Jubilee Junction?"

Susan shook her head. "I don't know. I hope not. As far as I know, there aren't any definite plans. I didn't want to tell you anything because all I know is that someone ordered the house to be cleared."

Aunt Violet turned towards us. "Someone tried to buy the property maybe thirty years ago. My husband was on the City Council. Turned out it was someone whose family moved away after their business failed in the thirties. Three generations later, they were looking for their roots and wanted to move back to town. They loved this property for its location near downtown, but they wanted to tear this place down and build a modern style house. They offered a generous amount, but no one dared bring it up to a vote. The local historical society would have had a fit. If they had the money, they would have already purchased it. But several of those city council men had mamas who belonged to the historical society."

As Aunt Violet talked, I closed my eyes and imagined this house in its glory days. I could almost hear the laughter of the children playing, the chatter of the quilting circle downstairs, and the hum of an old treadle sewing machine. I wished I had a time machine so I could see the house as it looked when Aunt Violet came here as a little girl to play. That gave me an idea.

I opened my eyes and turned to the group and said, "We need to raise the funds to save this house. It's the heart of so many stories, and we need to tell them."

I glanced around, and we all agreed.

Aunt Maggie smiled. "I'd like to help. What can we do?"

Kathy spoke up. "We could start a fund and call it Loaves and Fishes. Open a special bank account. Get some little donation cans for stores and restaurants."

Allie said, "A lot of local businesses might help. I know."

"I love that idea, Loaves and Fishes. Could we use the bookmark your grandmother Marie created? Could we tell the story of the quilting circle and the good they did during the Depression?" I asked. "Speaking of telling stories, we need to use social media to raise money. We could start a GoFundMe account, post a video tour, and interview people about the Great Depression."

Katie was on the verge of tears. "I'd like that."

I glanced around the attic. "Let me make some phone calls and get the college involved. The drama students could stage the place with a few trunks and some old toys—you know, make it look like it did when Mabel and Edward invited your great-grandma Edith and Marie, with her two little girls, into their home."

"Then stock this area with a chair, an old treadle sewing machine, and fabric on the shelves, patterns, sewing supplies, the works. Photography students can take pictures of the place, and marketing students could work with them to create the GoFund me page. They would also create signage for the house. Do some open houses and let people see it for themselves. Oh, and when I tell Carl about the situation, he'll want to help. The museum may have pieces to lend for the staging."

Tiara spoke up, "I could talk it up on my radio show, interview people, and even broadcast from the house."

Kathy looked around. "I could ask some of the high school teachers to help—and get their students involved. What better way to teach local history?"

Shelly nodded. "I love the idea. I'll help, Gracie!"

Mom added, "We could run a special insert in the newspaper, with pictures and a brief history of the house, calling for donations. We'd be happy to work with the college students."

Then she sat up a little straighter. "After I talk to Matthew and consult with our family lawyer, I believe we'll be visiting the mayor's office to talk about our proposal." She and Grandma Molly exchanged grins.

Grandma Molly's son, Uncle Joey, was the family lawyer. "I'll make sure that Joey is properly informed."

Susan looked around. "I'd love to save this old house, too. I can't imagine this street without it."

Aunt Maggie spoke up, "What about the special grants from the Founders Fund? Could we offer some money to help do the repairs and restoration? Would this qualify?"

Mom, Aunt Violet, and I all nodded.

Susan spoke up, "How would you all like to help us form a board to oversee the funding and restoration work? I can't think of anyone more qualified. You know the stories."

Charlotte spoke up, "I can help with research and help you locate things—like that old treadle sewing machine."

"That sounds good, but I think we also need your skills on our Loaves and Fishes Board, don't the rest of you agree? We wouldn't know some of these connections without you, Charlotte. Face it, you're part of my family now, just like Shelly and Tiara." I looked around.

My friend smiled, and Aunt Violet gave her a gentle hug.

Then I got out my notebook, and we went downstairs to sit on the couches in the parlor, and I made our first to-do list with lots of suggestions from Mom and Grandma Molly.

Thirty-one

The Holidays in Jubilee Junction, 1933
Marie

"Our little Loaves and Fishes group kept looking for people who needed our help and found them. Working together, we were able to offer a few folks a lending hand, a new dress, friendship, a cup of soup, or whatever we had to give."

~Marie

Autumn 1933

After a busy summer of sewing, quilting, and gardening, it is time for the girls to go back to school. Edith and I feel part of the church and community. It is good to have neighbors with children nearby. Jessie and Julia visit their friends living with Henny, and those children come to play at our house as well. My girls never lived so close to playmates before, and they loved it. Of course, Grace and Violet are part of the playtime.

The sisters are busy harvesting vegetables and canning them for the long winter. They've made jam and jelly, and their chatter and laughter fills the kitchen.

Our little Loaves and Fishes group kept searching for those folks who needed our help and found them. Working together, we were able to offer a few folks a helping hand, a new dress, our friendship, a cup of soup, a listening ear, or whatever we had to give.

Henny took Hazel to visit her lawyer son to get Hazel's divorce. While they were there, Henny also set up a fund for Hazel's kids. Henny's son was supportive, because his mother had been so much easier to deal with since Hazel moved in, and neighbors had stopped calling him to complain.

Henny's son brought his wife and son, who was now a sturdy toddler, to visit. Hazel and her children brought out some toys and her son, David, whispered in Henny's ear. Henny got down on the floor with a set of blocks. She stacked up three or four blocks, and her little grandson knocked them down, and they all laughed. Grandma Henny stacked up more blocks, and he knocked them down again and again. She laughed until she cried and then her daughter-in-law sat down and hugged her as she smiled at Hazel.

Hazel watched with delight. Later, she would tell us all about that moment. David had whispered, "Grandma Henny, babies like to knock down blocks."

As summer gave way to fall, I was wearing my maternity dresses and thankful that the nausea had passed. Most days I spent a few hours in the attic sewing room sewing clothes for those in need or for paying customers. People still dropped off sewing supplies and fabric from time to time.

In early October, our group completed the second Crazy quilt. Then Uncle Edward auctioned it off after church one Sunday. Verdeen was the high bidder. A few weeks later, we gave everyone their pillows and bookmarks, and they were plumb tickled. I had a feeling that the girls and I wouldn't be here forever, but these women were going to be my forever friends.

The quilt club volunteered to help organize two holiday meals at the church, one at Thanksgiving and one at Christmas. We would serve meals for anyone who needed it, and we encouraged those who could bring something to let us know.

I was also busy getting ready for our baby. We found a crib in the attic, so we carried it down, cleaned it up, painted it, and now it is in the corner of my bedroom. I sewed several little infant nightgowns, and someone gave me flour sack fabric for diapers.

As November arrives, Jessie and Julia are excited about the holidays and an upcoming school program.

"I must memorize a piece," Jessie tells me. "It's a Christmas poem, so I have to practice."

I nod. The girls are taking their baths and telling me about their day.

"I told Miss Helen we could bring some cookies. Is that alright?" Julia asks.

I assure her there will be sugar cookies for the program, scheduled for the week before Thanksgiving.

I stand and rubbed my big belly, smiling despite the ache in my back.

After tucking in the girls, I go downstairs to the dining room where Edith and Mabel sit at the dining room table planning the holidays along with Helen and Henny.

Thanksgiving had always been a simple family meal on the farm. We'd grown much of our own food, and the men would go hunting and bring home deer, rabbits, and squirrels.

This Thanksgiving potluck with the church will be a new experience for me, Edith, and the girls, and I was excited to hear more about it. Helen, Henny, and Aunt Mabel shared all about the traditional holiday festivities in Jubilee Junction.

"When it gets cold enough to freeze, people go ice skating on the river," Helen explains. "We always have skates to lend out."

Henny jumps in. "Afterward, we'll drink hot cocoa with marshmallows."

"We go caroling in downtown Jubilee Junction after Christmas Eve service," Mabel offers.

As I listen to all of them, I see my two girls peeking around the corner. The little scamps have sneaked out of bed and down the stairs. They have been listening, too, and can't contain their excitement. I beckon them to join us adults at the table.

Aunt Mabel assures them that there would be a Christmas tree. We'd decorate it with popcorn and cranberries strung on string, and add tinsel icicles. Mabel says she has a star for the top and a handful of bright red bulbs.

"Can we hang our stockings on the mantel?" Julia asks.

"It wouldn't be Christmas without it," Aunt Mabel assures her.

I send the little ones back to bed with the promise that I'll be up soon to tuck them in again, and the adults talk about what might go into those stockings. Carlson's General Store would have oranges for sale—a special treat in the middle of winter. I'd sewn new pajamas and purchased several toys at the store, including a set of eight houses in a Christmas village for sixty-nine cents. Mabel and Edith suggest knitting scarves and baking cookies for the festivities.

Uncle Edward, who has been whistling in his basement work-shop, passes by on his way to the attic. Before long he reappears, carrying something covered up with a sheet. I confess to being curious, but Uncle Edward just winks and starts whistling again on his way back to the basement.

As the days pass, I catch glimpses of Uncle Edward's mystery object while I am down in the cellar washing clothes in the Maytag wringer-washer. I can see something with a square base and an angled top, and a quick sniff discloses the presence of fresh paint.

Uncle Edward catches me peeking at it and lifts one side of the sheet to reveal a doll house, freshly painted.

"You're making doll furniture out of wood scraps? The girls will love it!" I say as he covers it back up.

In the evening after the girls have gone to bed, the sisters work on small objects that I soon realize are tiny dolls for the dollhouse in the basement.

The radio cheers us with Christmas music, but the news is sober-ing. Over twelve million people are still unemployed, thousands of farms lost to foreclosure, and families had abandoned their farms and homes and headed west. People are living in shanty towns built from packing crates, abandoned cars, and scraps of wood. Gangs of young men ride the railroads, searching for work. Churches and charities like the Red Cross set up soup kitchens and bread lines to help, but it only goes so far.

The radio announcer said folks who aren't near a soup kitchen will eat almost anything they can find to fill their bellies, including onion sandwiches, ketchup sandwiches, lard sandwiches—or just plain hog lard. Those with access to a rifle might hunt for rabbit or squirrel to add a bit of meat to their stew pot, or eat chicken feet in broth.

I almost gag at the idea of eating chicken feet. I'm just happy the girls are in school and don't hear these distressing details.

Edith and Mabel shake their heads and say, "Those poor folks."

Uncle Edward reads *The Jubilee Times* each week. He and I have had several conversation about what the new administration with President Roosevelt is doing to help. He had appointed Iowan Henry Wallace as the Secretary of Agriculture. Wallace was a corn scientist and editor of *The Farm Journal.* The federal government began sending checks to farmers to see if they'd reduce production of their crops. Uncle Edward approved of their plan.

"Maybe we can save a few farms." Uncle Edward looks almost wistful.

Aunt Mabel and Edith make me sit down and put up my feet several times a day, and they admonish Uncle Edward to make sure I don't get up and start working again.

By mid-November we'd already had several snowstorms coating fields and streams with snow.

The *Loaves and Fishes'* group is busy knitting stocking hats and mittens for children whose families couldn't afford to buy them.

We attend the school Christmas program and the children all do well. Edith, Mabel, Edward, and I sit and applaud as loudly as we can. Helen smiles proudly as she thanks the parents for coming to the program. We'd baked tray after tray of Christmas sugar cookies and serve them with tea, lemonade, and coffee for the adults.

Now it is time to get ready for our Thanksgiving Day meal, and I believe it is bound to be better than anyone can imagined because we were going to be together. We gather at the Methodist church, each family bringing something to the meal. Those who can't contribute food help cook, serve, and clean up. No one is left out at this festive feast.

I glance around the room full of church-goers enjoying the meal and feel a familiar ache of grief. Although my parents and sister have been dead for fifteen years, I miss them so much over the holidays. I seem to hear my mama's voice whispering gently, *Marie, let go of your grief. Your father and I—and your sister—will always be near.* My eyes fill with tears, and I whispered, "Mama, I love you."

Julia overhears and asks, "What did you say, Mama?"

I turn and say, "I love this chocolate cake!"

Julia nods and takes another bite of pumpkin pie as I nibble on Aunt Mabel's chocolate cake, savoring each bite. Jessie is giggling with Sarah and my heart is full of gratitude. We've found a home and an extended family. I look up and down at the quilting circle table. Henny's son, daughter-in-law, and little boy sit beside Hazel and her three children, and Henny is dishing up more macaroni and cheese for her grandsons. Six-year-old David is showing two-year-old Billie how to use a spoon to get the macaroni and cheese into his mouth.

"See. You did it!" he says, and everyone laughed. Then little Billy giggles and feeds himself another spoonful... and most of the food makes it into his little mouth.

Grace, Violet, and Mabel sit across from Jessie, Sarah, and Julia. They chat as they eat their dessert of choice—either pie or cake. Helen sits nearby and so do the rest of our quilters.

If only Frank were here.

Just as promised, the Jubilee River froze and there is ice skating with homemade skates that people are happy to share. Jessie and Julia find it great fun, but it makes me nervous, even though Aunt Mabel assures me it is safe. They only allow skating after the sheriff's office tests the ice to make sure it's at least four inches thick.

Henny, Hazel, Edith, and Aunt Mabel show the girls how to make marshmallows, using sugar, corn syrup, gelatine, hot water, vanilla, and cornstarch.

I hear lots of giggles as they stir the mixture on Mabel's stove. They take turns beating the candy until it is thick and stringy. They pour the sticky concoction into a pan and sprinkle confectioners' sugar on top. Now they must cut it into squares and let it sit overnight to dry off before packing it between layers of wax paper.

Last evening, we made a batch of hot cocoa and added a couple of marshmallows to each cup. The girls insisted they had never tasted anything so fine and drank every drop, giggling at each other's chocolate mustaches.

Uncle Edward observed them and nodded. "We're going to need more marshmallows, Mabel." His eyes twinkled.

Uncle Edward had cut down a Christmas tree and put it into a tree stand in the parlor. We began gathering cranberries, popcorn, and string for decorations. Aunt Mabel got out her star and half a dozen red bulbs. Uncle Edward lit a fire in the fireplace and helped the girls pop the popcorn in a long-handled popcorn popper.

Then began the fun of stringing the popcorn using large needles. I sat down on the horsehair couch to help.

Once the tree was done, we decorated the mantel with some small fragrant pine branches, candles, and stockings for the girls.

I wrapped the pajamas for the girls in newsprint and hid them in my room.

I felt enormous. The doctor says I'm doing just fine, and the baby's heartbeat is strong. In his letters Frank tells me he thinks I am carrying a little boy. I haven't gone up to the attic sewing room since the middle of December because I'm not feeling steady on my feet climbing up those attic steps. Of course, climbing down is even scarier!

The time came at last. Mabel, Ginny, Henny, Hazel, and Edith were there for me, and I gave birth at home to an adorable little baby boy. James Thomas Olson was born on December 25, the best Christmas gift I'd ever gotten. Frank and I had picked our son's name through letters: James after my father and Thomas for his uncle who died in WWI. Doctor Carlson came by the house to make sure both of us were healthy. Ginny, Henny, and Hazel watched the girls and made supper while Mabel and Edith stayed with me.

From the start, little James was a sweet-spirited boy spoiled by his sisters and everyone else. The quilt group gave us a baby shower, complete with sheets, a quilt, diapers, baby clothes, and a crocheted blanket.

Frank and Samuel have returned to meet the baby and see how we were doing. James is almost a month old now. Jessie is showing Papa Samuel how well she can read now from McGuffey's reader, while Frank is holding his son and crooning a little song as Julia is crowded up next to her daddy. I am as happy as I can be.

Edith takes the baby puts him down for a nap in his crib. The girl go off to play in the truck house with Papa Samuel, and Frank and I finally have time to just talk—and we had a lot to talk about.

Ginny has offered us a chance to be tenant farmers again when the men return for good, but while Frank thought about it and we discussed it, we both came to the same conclusion: "No, thank you kindly."

Frank was enjoying the construction work out West. As much as he had loved farming, having to walk away from his fields, animals, and equipment had taken its toll on him. He didn't think he could risk going through that again.

He and his father wanted to build truck houses, but first they were needed back in Wyoming for at least another season. Edith and I were saving the money they sent home for our new start even as we continued our *loaves and fishes* work, helping those who needed our help.

We celebrated two more Christmases in Jubilee Junction before Frank and Samuel came home for good. It was hard on our family, but Frank was proud to have helped train so many young men who desperately needed a second chance at life, teaching them new skills, and doing important work for their country.

Thirty-two

Leaving Jubilee Junction
Marie

"Brother, can you spare a dime?"

"As a young man, I lived through the Great Depression, when banks failed and so many lost their jobs and homes and went hungry. I was fortunate to have a job at a canning factory that paid 25 cents an hour."

~James E. Faust

Spring, 1936

*F*rank and Samuel have returned to Jubilee Junction in the truck house. We are so glad to see them. Photos and letters weren't enough. Little Jimmy has turned two and is walking, talking, and running. He and Uncle Edward are real close, and Edward has been mindful of always showed Jimmy photographs of his father and grandfather.

I am so thankful to have Frank back, and so are the girls, of course. Every night over supper, we hear more about their adventures out West, including all the wild animals they'd encountered. They'd seen some of them from afar, thankfully: black bears and bison, elk and deer, bighorn sheep and mountain goats, and prairie dogs.

Frank declares that they'd been amazed by the variations in the terrain of the state with rolling hills, then basins and mountains. They'd also made friends with people who had lived in Wyoming for a long time. Frank adds that Wyoming was the first state to allow women to vote and the first to elect a female governor: Nellie Tayloe Ross, 1925–1927.

Frank and Samuel talk to Edward about their ideas for the future. Every night after supper, they take over the big dining room table to talk. Uncle Edward pulls out his notepad and several pencils, and they all bend over some maps and talk intently.

During the past month, the three of men took off for several day trips. Edward took some vacation time off from the bank, and of course neither Frank nor Samuel were employed, so they didn't need to ask anyone's permission. When they came back from their last trip, they had exciting news. They'd purchased several plots of land with three houses and a large barn where they could build their truck houses. We were moving to western Illinois, just across the river.

And they had an even bigger surprise—Edward and Mabel were going with us!

Edward's heart wasn't in the bank anymore. The two incidents of violence had shaken him to his core. He realized he could've been gunned down in cold blood if Henny hadn't been there with her formidable pocketbook. He wanted to invest in the truck house industry. Besides that, Mabel missed her sister, and my children had become his grandchildren, too. So, they decided to move with us.

I knew it would be hard for Aunt Mabel to say goodbye to the quilting circle, especially her friends Ginny, Mildred, Henny, and Verdeen. But Hazel was joining the quilting circle to learn how to quilt, and so was her daughter Betsy. We knew the *loaves and fishes* ladies would continue to help people, and we determined to take the idea to Illinois, where maybe we could help people there, too.

We kept in touch, of course, writing lots of letters, and years later, talking on the telephone. We made occasional trips back to Jubilee Junction, usually for special events such as weddings—for Grace and Violet. They came to visit us, too. We grieved with them when Violet's twin Vera married Violet's boyfriend and had a baby with him before he died in the Second World War. What a mess that was, and how glad we were when Violet met that young doctor, who just swept her off her feet. Grace did real well, too, with that pilot. I could tell they were going to be happy when I saw the pictures Ginny sent.

Hazel stayed on with Henny after her children grew up and left home. She said she was done with men, but Henny just laughed and said her she was too young to be so foolish. Sure enough, a handsome man came along, a war veteran, and they married, and he moved in with Henny and Hazel.

My aunt and uncle sold their Queen Anne to the mayor, who promised to take good care of it. At its time, it was the most elegant home in town. We so enjoyed our stay there. I couldn't imagine someone else sleeping in those bedrooms and creating dresses in that attic sewing room. But that's how life is, isn't it? Change.

I cried when we drove away from the big Queen Anne in Jubilee Junction. Frank glanced over and grinned at me. "You'll love our large house in Peoria!"

He smiled at our girls, now almost eight and eleven, sitting between us as I held two-year-old Jimmy on my lap in our farm truck. We would need to go vehicle shopping once we got settled.

"Don't you girls ever forget that we lived here. Jubilee Junction was good to us in a terrible time. We're leaving behind lots of wonderful people, but they will be in our hearts, won't they?" I said, searching for my handkerchief in my sweater pocket.

Julia and Jessie gazed up at me. "I know, Mama. Grandma Edith told us the same thing last night, and she cried too. I told Grace and Sarah that I would write to them, and they promised to write back," Julia said.

Little Jimmy turned around on my lap. "Mama sad?" he said. "Hug."

I hugged my little boy. "Thank you, Jimmy. I feel better."

Frank caught my eye. "It's like my mother always said. Better days are coming."

And I thought, *He's right. They're here.*

Thirty-three

Violet's Recollection
Gracie

"Family stories matter. Share them so that your sons and daughters know who they are, and where we have come from."
~Aunt Violet

inally! It feels like we've pieced together the story and arranged a family meal. Katie invited her cousin Sarah to come, and we made sure the Crazy quilt is displayed so Katie's cousin can see it for herself. After the meal, we gathered in Mark and Kathy's large living room.

"I'm going to share what I've learned," I said, "and then Aunt Violet will tell us her memories of your grandmother, Jessie, was only five when she came to Jubilee Junction. The family had just lost their farm. Fortunately, her Aunt Mabel and Uncle Edward wanted to help. Their children were grown, so they had plenty of room in their large Queen Anne.

"Jessie didn't know that her mother had lost several family members during the 1918 Flu Pandemic. She was only familiar with her father's side of the family, the Olsons.

"In the spring of 1933, her grandparents and parents arrived in Jubilee Junction. They told the girls their grandfather Samuel and father, Frank, were going West to find work. Uncle Edward shared news about the CCC, a government program that would employ hundreds of thousands of young men. He was friends with the congressman from Iowa and had a cousin working in his office. He was able to get spots for them to work as supervisors out in Wyoming.

"So they left, driving that truck house, which attracted a lot of attention. Frank told Marie that the commander of the CCC camp had to come out and taken a tour. He said he would like to take a trip in something like that and was very intrigued.

"When they arrived, they felt shabby, and Aunt Mabel cleaned out some closets, with dresses left behind by her daughters. She shared some of her clothes with her sister. But she had a little attic sewing room, lots of fabric, and some patterns. So, Marie got to work sewing clothes, first for her little girls and herself, and then people hired her to make clothes for them. She always kept the leftover scraps in an old pillowcase. Your grandmother Marie and her mother-in-law, Edith, got involved with the community, church, and quilting circle.

"Julia, your grandmother's older sister, came home sad one day because one of her friends only had one dress to wear to school. The *Loaves and Fishes* project began when Marie used her earnings to buy shoes and clothes for that little girl. She also made things for the mother and her other children. Others in the quilting circle helped, and they helped many other families over the next two and a half years.

"A few weeks after Frank and Edward left, your great-grandmother discovered she was pregnant. While still living here, she gave birth to a baby boy named James, but they called him Jimmy. Edward and Frank came home for a visit to see the baby and then went back to work out West. Your family celebrated Christmas of 1933, 1934, and 1935 in Jubilee Junction. At last Frank and Samuel returned for good in the spring of 1936 with some plans.

"Uncle Edward had struggled during the banking crisis. He'd been a banker his entire adult life, but the wave of foreclosures was just too much for him. His heart wasn't in it anymore, and he ended up resigning in 1935. He and Mabel moved to Illinois with your family, and they set down roots there. But they always kept in touch with their friends back in Jubilee Junction.

"Now, let's hear from Aunt Violet."

I gestured to my aunt, and she glanced around the room and then told us what she remembered.

Aunt Violet's story:

"I was just a little girl, but I recollect meeting Marie and her girls at a quilt club meeting at the Queen Anne. Grace and I liked them right away. Marie was the mama, and the girls were Julia and Jessie. Julia was Grace's age, around eleven, and Jessie was a little younger than me, but we had fun playing together.

"Their grandmother Edith was Miss Mabel's sister. So, they were staying with their Aunt Mabel and Uncle Edward while their daddy and grandpa went West to work for the CCC.

"We went to school and church together and became friends. We met another little girl named Sarah and knew she needed help because she wore the same dress to school every day and the other kids made fun of her.

"Julia asked her mama to help, and the quilt club helped, too. One of them, Helen, was a teacher at the school, and knew Hazel, the mother.

"Mabel asked the family over for supper, and their neighbor, Henny, came too. Helen was there as well. Hazel was a young woman with three children and no family around. She was struggling and doing her best but needed a helping hand. Marie took each child and the mother aside to measure them for clothing.

"Julia said her mama had a magic pillowcase. It kept filling up with scraps as she kept getting more fabric to sew new dresses. She made dresses for Sarah and her mother and bought them shoes and coats. When we were little girls, we liked to think it was a magical pillowcase, of course.

"Henny was a widow who lived alone next door, and she took Hazel's family in when we found out they were living at the boarding house in one room. Their father had left them there and went West to find work with his brother, and they hadn't had a letter or any money from him in almost a year. So Hazel was cleaning houses to feed her children.

"Hazel was thankful for a better living situation. She got busy cleaning and cooking and kept Henny company, which made Henny happier. People said they heard laughter when they walked by her house. Her children—Betsy, Sarah, and David—loved Henny like she was their grandma, and it was good for everyone.

"The quilt group combined their scraps for a Crazy quilt to auction off for a new piano for the church. But people started dropping off their pillowcases full of scraps and the quilt group hand enough to make two Crazy quilts and then a bunch of pillows.

"Marie got this idea in her head that we could help people by working together, each person doing what he or she can. Then, God would reward our faith and supply what we needed, when we needed it, just like what happened when a little boy gave his lunch to Jesus. Jesus used it to feed a crowd of 5,000. His disciples passed around baskets full of *Loaves and Fishes.*

"I remember our mama explaining what it meant. If we'd use what we had, God would supply the rest. If we put our loaves and fishes together, we'd have enough. So, if the quilt ladies each brought their pillowcase full of fabric scraps, they'd have enough to create a Crazy quilt.

"What I remember from when we were all together before, is the Sunday church service where they auctioned off the first Crazy quilt. It was the most beautiful quilt I had ever seen, and the church was packed. After the sermon, Mr. Richardson, the banker, came up to do the auction.

"Then a man with a shotgun came into the church, and he marched down the aisle, towards the pastor and Mr. Richardson.

"I was sitting with Julia and Jessie, and we were terrified. Then Sarah's mama got right up and marched over to him. Hazel was hopping mad. Turned out it was her brother-in-law who had gone off with her husband almost a year ago.

"The young man pointed the gun at her and said he was going to blow a hole through her. But Henny picked up her big pocketbook and slugged him in the head. The would-be robber was just waking up when the deputy arrived to arrest him and march him out. The sheriff escorted Mr. Richardson to the bank with the money raised at the auction, but the church door had barely shut when there was a loud shotgun blast.

"Everyone ran to see what had happened. It was Hazel's absentee husband. He claimed he shot his own brother because he'd pointed the gun at Hazel. He tried to tell her he did it all for her. She didn't buy his story, and neither did her children.

"We were all a little shook up. Later, Mama asked Henny just what she had in her pocketbook that day, and it turned out Henny grabbed a brick on her way out of the door. She said she had a hunch. I guess it was a good one!

"We were in school together for two and a half years and Julia, Grace, Sarah, and I became the best of friends. We all liked to sit in that walk-in closet in their bedroom and pretend it was our own little house. And later, when Jimmy was born, we all just loved that little boy. He was too cute.

"I think your family left in the spring of 1936, and it was hard to say goodbye. We wrote letters, and we visited from time to time, driving over to Peoria to see those new truck houses.

"They sent photographs, and so did we, and Julia and Jessie just got prettier as they got older. I remember walking by the Queen Anne house on my way to visit Sarah. We missed those two little girls. We missed the Richardsons. They were good people. Years later, they came back for Grace's wedding and my wedding, too.

"I suspect you may never know completely why your grandmother Jessie didn't talk more about the past. Was it because her own mother, Marie, witnessed her whole family wiped out by the Spanish Flu in 1918? Was it because Uncle Edward didn't like to think about the violence that happened at the bank, and later at the auction? Was it because of the sorrow of losing that farm, or the family being separated from their grandfather and father? Or was it because she was a little girl growing up in Illinois? That's the funny thing about memories. They can be like quilts on your bed in wintertime, with the new ones just covering up the older ones."

Then Aunt Violet sat down and got out her hanky. Katie and her cousin were holding hands by now, and both were crying. David recorded it all for posterity.

Katie blew her nose and put her hankie away. "Oh my goodness. This is amazing. I can't believe all the information you found. I feel like I got to know my grandmother's family just now. It makes my photo album even more precious. I think it doesn't matter so much that I didn't know about the Jubilee Junction connection before, because I'm here now. It sounds crazy, but it makes me feel all the happier that Kathy married into this wonderful family."

Her cousin said, "Thank you for letting me hear this. I've had questions for years, and you've answered them. I didn't know any of this story. The photo album was a source of frustration since we didn't know the people, the location, or the meaning of the truck house, for example. How did you figure this all out besides your aunt?"

"Research using museum and library archives, genealogy databases, *The Jubilee Times,* and of course, Aunt Violet. The letters helped, and we found a journal that Marie kept. It's like doing a puzzle, but in real life you almost never get every piece. Then you have to guess a little." I grinned.

I handed both women a small flash drive and a printout of their family tree and some stories posted online by others in the extended family.

I handed Katie a bundle of letters. "These were very helpful. They're love letters from Frank to Marie and Marie to Frank. You have copies on the flash drives."

I was holding the album now with my gloves on.

"I'd really like to sit down with you right now and finish labeling all these pictures! You don't want the twins to find this old photo album some day and wonder who these people are, do you? Aunt Violet helped me identify most of the people and places—which explains all the sticky notes! It will mean the most to the twins if they recognize their grandma Katie's handwriting. Then we could post the pictures on Google photos."

Katie laughed. "Let's do it."

I handed them pens, and we got to work.

Thirty-four

Taking down the Tree
Gracie

"There were, of course, other heroes, little ones who did little things to help people get through: merchants who let profits disappear rather than lay off clerks, store owners who accepted teachers' scrip at face value not knowing if the state would ever redeem it, churches that set up soup kitchens, landlords who let tenants stay on the place while other owners turned to cattle, housewives who set out plates of cold food (biscuits and sweet potatoes seemed the fare of choice) so transients could eat without begging, railroad "bulls" who turned the other way when hoboes slipped on and off the trains, affluent families that carefully wrapped leftover food because they knew that residents of "Hooverville" down by the dump would be scavenging their garbage for their next meal, and more, and more. But they were not enough, could not have been enough, so when the government stepped in to help, those needing help were thankful."
~Harvey H. Jackson

The day after the "big reveal," as David liked to call it, we were taking down our decorations inside. I couldn't stand the tree any longer—its apple cider vinegar smell was pungent, and not in a fresh clean pine way, either. We were going to take it out of the house and then figure out a nice way to recycle it, far away from the front porch.

Agatha perched on top of her cat tree, watching.

I had our storage boxes out and ready for the new tree decorations.

I had a trash can for the orange peels and foil. I put on my kitchen gloves and stripped the tree of its decorations and defensive materials.

I called David, and he helped me maneuver the tree out the front door. We stopped to assess the trail of pine needles.

"Let's just get it off the porch," I begged.

David grinned. "I've been doing research online and there are a lot of things you can do with a Christmas tree."

I knew that look. "You want to chop it up for firewood?" I asked, skeptical.

"No. I have a few other ideas," he said. "Let's just prop it up against the garage."

So we did, and he headed for his workbench with his iPad and trusty *Popular Mechanics* magazine. I sighed.

We were keeping our outdoor decorations up for weeks. We loved driving home and seeing them turn on, thanks to the timer my handy husband had installed.

I turned around to go back to the house, to deal with the mess left behind when my cell phone rang. It was Katie.

"Hi Gracie. My cousin just left. We had the best talk. She wanted me to thank you again for checking into the Crazy quilt pictures in my grandma's album. I feel great today, and I don't know if it's karma or a God thing, but now I know Ken and I are meant to be here in Jubilee Junction. You said the twins are the eighth generation to grow up here, which is amazing. I keep thinking, eighty years ago, my grandmother came here as a little girl and was friends with your Grandma Grace and Aunt Violet. Knowing your family stories makes all the difference. I want to be sure to pass them on to Sophie and Sean."

"Oh, Katie, that's wonderful. You're welcome. We enjoyed doing the research and hearing Aunt Violet tell stories about Grandma Grace and Violet as little girls."

We said goodbye, and I went over to where the tree had been and found Agatha sniffing at the few pine needles with a very annoyed expression on her face.

I found my Febreze—pine fresh—and sprayed a few times until I couldn't smell the apple cider anymore.

Agatha scampered away when she saw the spray bottle of Febreze

I laughed and cleaned up the mess. Then I finished putting the ornaments back in place in their boxes and carried them down to the basement.

I grabbed the baby gate and bag of trash and walked toward the door. I closed the bag of trash and set it outside and then took the baby gate downstairs to the furnace room.

As I headed back upstairs, I thought of the stories about the truck house that Samuel and Frank built together. I wondered what it had been like to travel like that, back during the Depression. For its time, it was a remarkable invention and attracted a lot of attention. I thought about our honeymoon trip in Uncle Rich's RV. What would Samuel and Frank have thought of it? David and I had certainly enjoyed driving cross country in the Greyhawk. I wondered what adventures the new year would bring?

Mom had fast tracked our Queen Anne house rescue, as she was calling it, by setting up a bank account after talking to the mayor with Dad. He and Dad had gone to school together. Mom had also called Uncle Joey for advice. He was looking into setting up a nonprofit so that donations would be tax deductible. We were going to meet after the holidays, but we'd already gotten the museum, historical society, library, and college onboard. Aunt Violet was thrilled, and I was happy to be in her good graces again.

Uncle Vern had called to make sure that I was okay with him visiting Jimmy Joe. "I think he wants to apologize to you and Mark, and your parents, for his actions. Let's talk more about it after the new year."

I'd assured him I was fine. We'd talk more. As we said goodbye, I realized something had shifted in my thinking. Seeing a humbled Jimmy Joe at church on Christmas Eve had helped me see him the way Uncle Vern had—as a man who lost his way after his wife died. As a man with regrets, haunted by choices made that only made things worse. As a man feeling guilty for the death of his daughter-in-law, depriving his grandson of his mother. As a man who had doubted his wife's assessment of their son's problems with alcohol and violence and then lived to regret his actions. Yes, he'd done some terrible things to my family, but I no longer was afraid of him. He was a man in need of redemption. Weren't we all?

As I walked back into the living room, Agatha was running around in circles, overjoyed to have the stinky tree gone. Truth be told, I was glad to have it gone, too.

I picked her up, sat down on the couch, and gave her some attention.

"Does it smell better now, Agatha? I overdid it with the apple cider vinegar, and I'm sorry." I stroked her back just the way she liked it. She purred and must have forgiven me because she cuddled up in my lap and licked my fingers.

All was right with the world. I smiled at the thought. We still had the weekend. Maybe David and I could finally relax.

The Sacrifice
Grandmother's Treasures, Book Five

 atie's cousin, Sarah, who lives in Illinois, finds a box with a set of cassette tapes—sent from Grandma Grace to Marie in Illinois and an unfinished quilt meant for Richard, Junior, going back to the mid-1970s at the end of the war in Vietnam.

On their way to the first day of the Spring semester's meetings, Gracie and David come upon a horrific accident, rescue an infant, and call for help for the child's parents who are both seriously injured.

These two seemingly unrelated events soon intertwine with stories of war, trauma, and recovery.

Bonus Material

Cast of Characters

The Contempory Cast

Gracie O'Connor MacNeill—the main character, a young teacher who works at the county museum part-time and writes for the family newspaper

David MacNeill—her husband, a young history teacher at Jubilee Junction Community College

Matthew and Becky O'Connor—Gracie's parents. Matthew is the editor of *The Jubilee Times*, a weekly newspaper, where Becky is the business manager.

Great Aunt Violet Johnson—Becky's aunt

Mark O'Connor, his wife, Kathy O'Connor, and their twins Sophie and Sean—Mark is Gracie's brother

Katie and Ken Daniels—Kathy's parents, who move to Jubilee Junction when they discover Kathy's expecting twins

Uncle Vern and Aunt Maggie—Becky's aunt and uncle

Shelly Kellogg—adjunct at Jubilee Community College. She and Gracie have been friends since elementary school

Tiara Butler—adjunct in the English at Jubilee Community College who teaches speech and hosts a radio show

Carl Patten—Director of the county museum

Charlotte Lewis-Garcia—Librarian, Jubilee Junction Public Library

James Joseph Flett (aka Jimmy Joe)—the White supremacist who rammed his truck into Mark and Kathy's house

Roselyn and Roxanne—Jimmy Joe's daughters. Their husbands are Roger and Scott respectively.

Harold Jenkins—Donna's husband.

Julie Jenkins—Donna's daughter and Vera's granddaughter.

Aunt Shirley Carlson—Becky's cousin, runs the Jubilee Café in Jubilee Junction with her family.

The Historical Cast

Marie Olson and her husband, Frank—farmers

Jessie and Julia—Marie and Frank's daughters

Samuel and Edith Olson—Frank's parents, farmers

Aunt Mabel and Uncle Edward Richardson—the banker in Jubilee Junction.

Ginny Nelson—Mabel's best friend, Practical, strict, loving

Grace and Violet—two of Ginny's daughters

Verdeen Carlson—Ginny's sister. Speaks her mind, can be critical

Irene O'Connor—Verdeen's friend.

Her son, James, is The Jubilee Times editor

James O'Connor—son of Irene and editor of The Jubilee Times

Henrietta "Henny" Carlson—Eccentric but warmhearted and a little bored

Mildred Jones—married to the preacher, Rev. Martin Jones. Friendly and warm, talkative

Helen Johnson—School teacher. Single, lonely

Hazel—a young woman abandoned by her husband, living in one room in the boarding house with her three children, Miriam, Sarah, and David

Sarah—Hazel's daughter. She becomes friends with Julia, Marie's daughter.

The Story Behind the Story

My mother told me stories about this truck house; her father, Lee Lewis, built it on the back of one of his large farm trucks. The old bench was inside to store some of their supplies.

Lee, Nellie, and his mother, Eva, along with my mother and her two sisters, rode in the truck house out West to California in the late 1920s, stopping in Arizona for a few months. They stayed in a little camp, and the girls went to school while Lee dug irrigation ditches. They went to the Grand Canyon and on to California, getting stuck at least once and needing another truck house to pull them out!

Grandma Nellie's Sugar Cookies

*T*his recipe goes back to Nellie Lewis Egger, my maternal grandmother, a rural Iowa farm wife. Remembered for her sweet personality, love of her grandchildren, her love of nature, and flowers—especially roses—and wonderful cooking and baking. She always said she would rather make a pie than a cake. She kept a variety of 12-ounce glass bottles of orange, strawberry and grape pop—a special treat when we visited. She taught Cherie to walk on stilts when Nellie was 65, wrote poetry, sang gospel songs to us, and loved to swing in the weeping willow tree's swing in her front yard.

Dust and dirt were her enemy and living on a little farm off a gravel road made housekeeping a challenge, even with her mud-room right inside the back door. Grandma swept off Grandpa Art's overalls with a broom before allowing him back into her house. Grandma put dirty dishes into the oven when she saw company driving down the road! We teased her later that she was trying to invent the dishwasher.

I remember making these cookies with her as a small child: smelling them in the oven and wiggling with delight, in anticipation of eating that first cookie. I've made them almost every Christmas of my adult life. When I visit my sister Cathi or cousin Charlene during the holidays, we always ask, "So have you made any of Grandma Nellie's sugar cookies yet?"

I prefer them thin and crispy; however, they soften if frosted. My son, Jon Post, a much better baker than I am, makes them softer by not baking them as long. Either way, they're wonderful.

Ingredients
2 cups sugar
½ cup shortening (butter Crisco works well)
1 stick margarine
3 large eggs
3 tablespoons milk
3 teaspoons baking powder
2 teaspoons vanilla
3 cups flour (plus more as needed)

Directions
Mix shortening, margarine, and sugar with mixer until creamy.
Add eggs, milk and vanilla—mix well.
Add the rest of the ingredients and mix well.
Refrigerate the dough for a few hours; it will be much easier to work with if you can chill it overnight.

Work with dough in small amounts; if it seems too sticky, add additional flour. Put down some flour on the counter and roll it out to the desired thickness (thicker cookies bake softer; thinner will be crispier) and use your favorite cookie cutters.

Bake for 8–9 minutes at 350; depending on your preference, thicker cookies may take an additional minute or two.

One batch makes several dozen cookies, depending on the size of the cookie cutters.

Note
This recipe works well when doubled. I don't think that I have ever made a single batch! However, when doubled, it is even more important not to cheat on letting the dough chill, even if only for several hours. I often let it sit overnight in my largest Tupperware bowl in the refrigerator.

Amish Sugar Cookies

$\mathcal{I}$ got this recipe back in the 1970s from a military wife out in Newport, Rhode Island. They're easy, yummy, and have crinkly edges. I like them plain, but I've also sprinkled red and green sprinkles on them.

Ingredients
1 cup sugar
1 cup powdered sugar
1 cup butter or margarine
1 cup cooking oil
2 eggs
41/2 cups flour
1 tsp. baking powder
1 tsp. baking soda
1 tsp cream of tartar
1 tsp vanilla

Directions
Combine the sugars, butter, and oil; beat well. Add eggs and mix well. Add dry ingredients and mix well with an electric mixer.

Make into small balls and flatten slightly with a small juice glass or fork; sprinkle on a little sugar or holiday sprinkles for color.

Bake at 375 for 10–12 minutes.

One batch makes 4–5 dozen, depending on the size of the scoop. I can't recall ever making a single batch.

When I taught at Hawkeye Community College, I almost always made these cookies and took them to classes around the holidays.

Note
   This recipe works best if you chill the dough overnight.

180

Chocolate Depression Cake

*T*his unique Chocolate Cake recipe, popular-
ized during the great depression, is rich and chocolate without the
using any eggs, butter, or milk!

Time Requirement
Prep Time, 15 minutes
Cook Time, 35 minutes
Cooling Time, 1 hour

Ingredients
Chocolate Cake
1.5 cups all-purpose flour
1 cup granulated sugar
1/2 tsp salt
1 tsp baking soda
1/3 cup unsweetened cocoa powder
1/3 cup cooking oil*
1 Tbsp vinegar**
1 tsp vanilla extract
1 cup water
Chocolate Icing
1.5 cups powdered sugar
1/4 cup cocoa powder
3 Tbsp water
1 tsp vanilla extract

Instructions

Chocolate Cake

Preheat the oven to 350ºF. In a large bowl, stir together the flour, sugar, salt, baking soda, and cocoa powder until well combined.

Add 1 cup water to a liquid measuring cup, then add the vanilla extract and vinegar to the water.

Add the oil to the bowl of dry ingredients, followed by the water mixture. Stir until the chocolate cake batter is mostly smooth. Make sure no dry flour remains on the bottom of the bowl.

Pour the cake batter into an 8x8" or 9x9" baking dish. Transfer the baking dish to the oven and bake the cake for 35 minutes.

Chocolate Icing

If using the chocolate icing, let the cake cool for at least an hour after baking before adding the icing.

Wait until the cake is cool, then prepare the icing. Add the powdered sugar, cocoa powder, and vanilla extract to a bowl. Begin adding water, 1 tablespoon at a time, until it forms a thick but pour-able icing (about 3 Tbsp total). If you let the icing sit, it may begin to dry, but you can add a splash more water to make it moist again.

Pour the icing over the cooled cake and spread until the cake is evenly covered. Slice the cake into 9 pieces and serve.

Notes

*Use any neutral cooking oil of your choice, like canola, vegetable, grapeseed, safflower, corn, or avocado oil.

**Any light vinegar will work, like white vinegar, rice vinegar, or apple cider vinegar.

Acknowledgements

No one writes a novel, let alone a series, without help. This adventure has given me the opportunity to use my family's cherished quilts and tidbits of our family history. It's also given me the chance to think like one of my favorite authors, Ruth Suckow, and say, "What if?"

I thought I might be done with three books. Then it was as if my characters were talking to me. Wouldn't it be fun to see Grace and Violet as little girls growing up during the Great Depression? The more I thought about it, I remembered a couple of Crazy quilts and flour sack towels in my stash of family linens.

My mother, Charlotte, the middle daughter, took care of Grandma Eva and then her mother, Nellie. She inherited a dozen or more quilts, storing them in her bedroom above the closet. Later, she put them into a large wooden chest her father built back in the early 1920s, the one that is now in my office. She was a writer who encouraged me to scribble my stories as a little girl. She created little booklets by folding typing paper in half and stapling them.

In her retirement years, she reconstructed her young adult years by corresponding with Bruce, a childhood friend. They came of age right before WWII, so I found essays/chapters dated 1939 through 1946 and she had the most incredible details woven into each chapter: the price of dresses, the highlights of the war with the battles, losses, and her work as a riveter helping to build the flying fortress bombers that helped win the war. Mother, you inspired me, and your little sister, Jeanne, was my cheerleader in chief.

Then I realized that Book Three was ending right before the holidays. Wouldn't it be fun to write a Christmas novella about

Gracie and David's first Christmas as a married couple, now living out in the country in one of the family farmhouses?

No sooner had I come up with a story for Book Four than I realized I had an idea for *Book Five: The Sacrifice*, with a very dramatic opening scene. Since then, Mike and I have dreamed up at least three more novels.

To my husband, who serves as fact checker, beta reader, and researcher, thank you, Mike!

To my best friend Beth, my first Beta reader during Covid, thanks for encouraging me. "Every book gets better!" We talk every Wednesday night, and I remember you saying that with each new book.

To my friend and a new Beta Reader, Ambri, thanks for pushing me to find the Christmas story set during the Great Depression.

To the others who read an early draft—Judith, Mikki, Barbara, and Joy—thank you for your feedback and encouragement.

To my illustrator, Patricia, thanks for your help with each book. I love the maps, the bookmarks, and the QR codes you create.

To my publisher, Mike Parker, thank you for your gift of finding/creating the perfect covers for each book.

Connect with me online at:

cheriedargan.com
facebook.com/CherieDarganAuthor/
substack.com/@cheriedargan

Invite me to visit your book club

I'm available for face to face and online meetups via Zoom or Google Meet. Contact me, cheriedargan@gmail.com

Cherie Dargan

After nearly 30 years in education and 20 years teaching writing, literature, and educational technology courses at Hawkeye Community College, Cherie took early retirement in 2016. She joined the Cedar Falls Authors Festival planning committee, celebrating the five best-selling writers with ties to Cedar Falls—Bess Streeter Aldrich, Ruth Suckow, James Hearst, Robert Waller, and Nancy Price.

Cherie contributed two chapters for collections of academic essays: one about Iowa writer Ruth Suckow and the other about the literary history of Cedar Falls, Iowa. She is the author of the *Grandmother's Treasures* series, including *Book 1 The Gift, Book 2 The Legacy, Book 3 The Promise, and Book 4 The Recollection* with one more volume in the works.

She serves as the past president, historian, and program chair of the League of Women Voters of Black Hawk-Bremer Counties advocating for voting rights for all. She is Mom to four children and Grandma to three grandchildren. Cherie is married to retired librarian Mike Dargan, who serves as her tech support, fact checker, and head cheerleader.